CASSIE MINT

Teacher's Pet

BLACK CHERRY
PUBLISHING

Contents

Keep in touch with Cassie!

Want to stay up to date with new releases, sales, and more instalove goodness?

Sign up for Cassie's newsletter!

1

Love Lessons

Description

One year ago, I saw her in my class.

One year ago, the ground opened up beneath me.

Avery Jennings. She's my student. My secret longing. My kryptonite. After I taught her for one semester, I was clear: she needs to stay away. My restraint is wearing thin.

But the first day of class in her second year, who do I find in my lecture hall?

Avery is sweet. Determined. She looks at me with hearts in her eyes.

And I'm a monster. A wicked man. Because with her... I can't resist.

Avery

I rush across campus, my backpack bouncing and my class schedule clutched to my chest. My sandals slap against the hot paving stones, baked all summer long, and I gasp for breath as I sprint across the quad. My sundress floats around my thighs, my hair streaming behind me, and other students mutter and step out of the way as I barrel through them.

I'm late. *Late.* This wasn't the plan. When I woke up this morning, teeth gritted with purpose, *this* wasn't what I had in mind. It took me all summer to build up my courage, to sign up for Professor Kent's class, and this is how he'll find out? When I burst into the lecture hall five minutes late, red faced and wheezing?

Kill me now.

I'm rushing so fast, I almost sprint right past the English building. I skid to a halt, arms pinwheeling, then duck past a group of staring grad students to push through the doors.

A clock hangs opposite the entrance, ticking my seconds away. Two minutes until the first class of the semester starts.

Two minutes until I'm late.

Until I see *him.*

I check the schedule crumpled in one fist, smoothing it out with shaking fingers. My breaths come quick and loud as I read the room number, sending up a silent prayer of thanks.

It's just here. The nearest lecture hall, tucked around the corner.

I'm going to make it.

I smooth my wild hair down. Tug on the hem of my dress. Swipe my forearm over my dewy forehead, my skin flushed hot from running. Then give myself my third pep talk of the day.

You can do this, Avery Jennings. Now get your ass in that room.

It's pretty basic, as pep talks go. Nothing like the elaborate mantras in the self help books I've been reading all summer. But it does the trick: I square my shoulders, hitching my backpack higher, and march around the corner to the lecture hall. I don't break stride, pushing the door open and plunging inside. The rows are two-thirds full, with students laughing and leaning past each other to catch up. They call out nicknames; toss balled up class schedules at each other's heads.

I don't even see them. Not really. I drift to an empty seat in the third row, the din around me fading to nothing, and sit down clumsily.

He's here.

Professor Kent stands at the lectern on the raised platform at the front of the room. He stares at me, white-faced, his hands gripping the lectern so tight that I can almost hear the wood creak.

Even though it's another hot, sticky day, he's wearing a white button down shirt with only the top button undone. The fabric fits him perfectly, hugging his toned shoulders and nipping in with his slender waist, and it's not just the heat that makes my mouth run dry when I look at him.

God. Professor Kent is a walking dirty daydream.

One of his dark curls hangs over his forehead, and he presses his mouth in a tight line. His gaze rakes over me where I sit, just as hungry as I remember, and he swallows. Hard.

A bell rings out in the corridor. The last student to enter slams the door shut, a steady hush falling over the crowd, and now we're trapped here. Together at last, for the next sixty minutes.

He's annoyed. Distracted. I've thrown him off his usual self assurance, the deep confidence which makes so many of the students sigh. Professor Kent throws one final irritated glance at me, clears his throat, and begins.

Shakespearean Literature. It's not really my thing. It's not *his* thing either, but I'm not supposed to know that. I shouldn't be able to read his moods the way I do. I took this class for one reason alone, and he's currently gripping the lectern like he might crush it to splinters.

His calm voice belies the tension rigid in his body as he introduces the class. Highlights key dates and assignments. Gives reading lists.

Macbeth. Romeo and Juliet. The Taming of the Shrew.

Yes, fine. Whatever. I'll read whatever plays this man assigns. I'll hand in all the assignments; do every scrap of suggested reading.

Anything, to finally be near him again. To hear his deep, melodic voice. To feel the heavy weight of his gaze on me.

I'm not as strong as Professor Kent. Or—or I *am,* but this is a different kind of strength. One I've been building up all summer with my mantras and self help manuals.

I won't hide from my feelings. Won't pretend that I don't feel his presence from fifty feet away; that I don't forget to breathe whenever his gray eyes land on me.

Professor Kent haunts my dreams.

And I can't stay away anymore.

* * *

"A moment, please, Miss Jennings."

His stern voice cuts through the din as the students file out of their rows, chatting about their next classes. I have a free period, but even if I didn't there's no way I'd be shuffling out that door. Not yet.

I nod and grab my backpack, not daring to meet his eyes as I zip away my notebook and push to my feet. All the confidence that buoyed me here—it's draining fast. Oh god, will he hate me for this?

"Hi, professor." My words come out in a whisper as I step up onto the stage. Professor Kent keeps his head bowed, his square jaw clenching as he packs away his notes. I shift my weight, biting my lip.

He waits until the last student leaves the room. Until the door bangs shut, the sound echoing through the huge space. Then he turns to me, eyes molten, and hisses his question.

"Avery. What are you doing here?"

"Learning about Shakespeare," I mumble. He jerks his head to the side, annoyed. He knows I don't care about Shakespeare. That's the problem, really—we can read each other entirely too well for professor and student.

"Cut the crap." I wince, and he scrubs a hand over his face.

He's agitated. More out of control than I've ever seen him. "I told you last year. One class was enough. This isn't—this is a bad idea. Do you understand?"

I scowl down at his chest. His shirt is perfectly pressed. Does he do that himself? Or does he have a wife or girlfriend who does it for him? Jealousy crawls through my stomach, sickly and slow.

"I'm here to learn," I grit out, eyes burning, my gaze fixed on that top button. It's a lie, but all the pretty speeches I rehearsed, all the declarations I had planned—they've evaporated like fine mist. And besides, I don't *want* to tell Professor Kent how much I love him when he's being an ass. So there.

"Forget it. I'm taking you to change your classes right now." He grabs my elbow, then drops it just as fast. Like he's been stung. I huff and cross my arms, walking ahead of him off the platform.

"You can't force me to switch."

"I can, actually. I can transfer you for bad behavior. I can fail you outright. You're leaving, Avery."

I wrap my arms around my waist tighter. This is not what I'd imagined, all those long nights of planning over the summer. I knew he'd be surprised. Maybe taken aback.

I never dreamed he would be cruel. And the pain of his harsh words—it cuts right through me. Right down to the bone. Tears sting my eyes, and before I can help it, my breath catches right here in the silent lecture hall.

"Wait." His command comes from behind me. I keep walking, my sandals slapping against the tiled floor. "Avery. Are you crying?"

The door is heavy as I wrench it open. I keep my spare arm wrapped around my waist, holding my insides together.

"Avery," he says again, more desperate this time. I step through the doorway and into the corridor.

It's cooler out here. Shadowed. I duck my face and hurry far away from Professor Kent.

Ellis

Avery whips through the lecture hall doorway, disappearing into the corridor. I lunge after her, slamming the door open so hard that it bounces off the wall, but she's already gone. Groups of students cluster together by the walls, laughing and joking, a few of them throwing me odd looks.

It's the beginning of the semester. They're not burned out and exhausted yet. They still have that post-summer glow about them, their futures bright and exciting.

All except Avery. Yeah, I dimmed her light pretty fast.

I grit my teeth as I stride down the corridor, peering into empty classrooms and searching for a flash of light blonde hair. She wore it in a French braid today, the ends tickling her shoulders. She *knows* I like it like that. That cute little sundress, with the daisy print and the flippy skirt—was that for my benefit too? I stifle a groan, rubbing my jaw.

No. It wasn't for me. Thoughts like those—they're why I can't be around her. Why I can't be trusted to teach Avery Jennings.

I'd never keep my hands off her. Not for another semester. I don't have the strength.

Last year was the hardest year of my life. Of my brief but esteemed career. I only taught Avery in the first semester, but that one class was enough. I spent the rest of the year white-knuckling through until the summer.

Until I could get some distance from her, some reprieve from her constant presence on campus. The flash of her bright hair. The tinkling sound of her laugh.

Avery Jennings is my own personal torment. She haunts my every waking moment—and my dreams, too.

I've never touched her. That's my only saving grace. The only reason I don't march myself to the Dean's office and hand myself in. I've touched *myself* thinking of her, sure, jerked my cock until it's raw, but I've never laid a finger on Avery Jennings.

She knows I want to. She can read it on my face. And she *goads* me to do it, the little tease. I'd think she's out to ruin me, that this is all a big joke to her, but her wide blue eyes are innocent. Guileless. She doesn't understand the effect she has. How frayed my tether has become.

I understand it. I know it all too damn well. And I *know*, in the dark, bitter depths of my soul, that if I teach her for another semester, there's only one way it will end. In ruin. In madness. With my cock buried to the hilt inside her, and Avery crying out my name.

Which leaves me no choice but to transfer her out of my class. She doesn't even *like* Shakespeare, damn it.

I push out of the English building doors and stride across campus. Energy crackles under my skin, keeps my muscles tensed and my jaw locked, but I don't catch another glimpse of her.

Hi, professor.

She sounded so shy. Like she thought I might bite her sweet head off.

And I did, didn't I? I told her off. Threatened to fail her. God—I made her cry. Misery and self loathing surge up my throat, and I cough hard, burying my mouth in my sleeve.

The sun is shining. The students are laughing. But I'm icy cold, down to my core. Hearing that little hitch in Avery's breathing, her tiny sniffle—it's going to haunt the rest of my days. It'll play in a loop inside my head, driving me slowly mad.

How Shakespearean.

It doesn't matter. I give myself a little shake, and turn my feet towards the Student Center. I'll get her transferred to another class, then we can both move on. Put this behind us and somehow get through the next three years.

Then she'll be gone. We'll both be safe from these dark urges, rippling and twisting inside me.

It should be a comforting thought. But it *aches.* It leaves me hollow.

I pound up the stone steps to the Student Center, pigeons fluttering out of my path. It doesn't matter what *I* want.

This is for Avery. I'd protect her from anything.

Even myself.

* * *

"Please. Will you look again? I'll take any other class. I'm begging you."

I recognize her soft voice straight away. She's clutching the

12

edge of the reception desk, pleading with the administrator. Her shoulders are rigid, bunched up around her ears, and her voice is thick with horror at what I just put her through.

She's begging to get away from me. My heart plummets down to the soles of my shoes.

"I already looked." The administrator sounds bored. It's a guy in his twenties, probably a grad student picking up some work-study hours, and violence surges inside me when his eyes flick over her chest. He looks at her openly. Shamelessly.

She's *mine.*

"Is there a problem here?" I stride across the lobby, coming to a halt beside Avery. I don't look down at her—I don't trust myself not to crumble under her gaze. To not drop to my knees and beg her forgiveness. She freezes when I'm near, the tension crackling off her like static, and *fuck*, I hate that I did this.

I channel all those feelings at the administrator. He straightens, his forehead creasing as he taps at his keyboard. His brown hair is artfully tousled, sticky with gel, and if he looks at her again I might go for his throat.

"Uh, no. No, sir. This girl wants to switch classes, but there are none available."

Shit.

"Check again."

"But—"

"Check again," I growl, ignoring the faint whimper by my elbow. She might hate me, might fear me, but that's all for the best. Even if it does crack my chest open and leave me raw.

The administrator types quickly, clicks away at the screen, then spins the monitor around with a huff.

"There's nothing. See?"

I lean over the counter, scowling at the class schedules. How can every class be full already? *How can this be happening?*

"What about night classes?" I blurt, but Avery speaks up. Her voice is tight with emotion, but she doesn't back down.

"No. I'm not doing that, professor." She sucks in a deep breath and fixes me with a glare. I meet her eyes, longing shuddering through me like a tidal wave. "You'll just have to teach me."

"I—what?" The guy breaks off with a nervous laugh. His eyes flick between us, disbelieving.

I step away from Avery. Put more distance between us.

"It's nothing," I mutter, turning to face her. The girl who wrecks me with a single look. Who holds my whole life in her palm. "I expect you on time for lectures. Do you understand?" She was nearly late today. That would have thrown me off even worse. Given me no time to recover.

Avery rolls her eyes, a pink flush creeping over her cheeks.

"Don't worry about me, professor." Her voice is dull. "You won't even know I'm there."

She walks out before I can point out the obvious. That if *that* were true, we'd have no problem at all. But I'm human, a man, and I'm drawn to her like no other person. Every minute in her presence is a test of my failing willpower.

"Wow. You really hate her, huh?" The administrator grins, flicking his mouse.

I turn on my heel and leave without a word.

Avery

I've made such a terrible mistake.

As soon as I got home on that first day of classes, I stomped upstairs, snatched up all my self help books, and threw them in the trash can. Leona and Paige, my roommates, came poking their heads into my bedroom, fussing over my flushed cheeks and watery eyes.

"Oh, Ave!" Paige stumbled into my room, wrapping me in her tiny arms. Paige is a ballet dancer, so small that she looks like she might blow away. "It didn't go well with the professor?"

I shook my head, teeth gritted. "He didn't want me there. He tried to force me to transfer. Threatened to fail me if I didn't."

Paige gasped, shocked, but Leona cocked her head where she leaned against the door frame.

"It bothered him, then." I shrugged. She smirked. "So he *does* care."

I can't think of it like that. I spent the whole summer break kidding myself that Professor Kent and I really had something.

All those mantras about going after what I want, all those long, hot summer nights slipping my hand into my pajama shorts and thinking of him…

It's humiliating.

How did I get this so wrong?

The second class, I'm better prepared. I know now how he'll look at me: like a nuisance. Like a chore he has to deal with. So I arrive ten minutes early, armed with a giant takeout iced coffee, and climb all the way to the back row. Professor Kent isn't here yet—I hope he never comes, the jerk—but when he arrives, he'll have no reason to even notice me.

I tug my black baseball cap down over my eyes, slink low into my seat, and lever open my laptop.

Perfect. Between the cap and my laptop, only an inch of my face shows.

I get a few weird looks when the other students file in, flopping down in the seats like it's the crack of dawn and not 10am. But I force a smile for anyone who looks my way, and soon enough, I blend into the background. Once the rows fill with bodies, I'm invisible.

Or I thought I was. The second Professor Kent walks through the door, his gaze tracks to me. Fixes on the sliver of my face that he can see. I huff, sliding lower until my chin is on my chest and I'm completely hidden by the laptop.

"Nap time?" A guy a few seats over grins at me. I shrug, a smile tugging my mouth.

"I had a late night," I whisper. I don't mean anything by it, but the guy lights up. Like because I mentioned *night time*, I must have meant *come nearer*. He slides over until he's sat in the seat next to mine, propping his elbow on the desk and staring right at me.

Um. Hello? Professor Kent is about to begin the lecture. And he does, his low voice cutting through the whispers. Everyone quiets down, shuffling in their seats. Even my nosy neighbor turns around, opening his laptop.

Everyone knows better than to piss off Professor Kent. Not because he's a jerk—other than to me, apparently. But because he's strict. Kind of a hard ass. He won't suffer fools.

I loved that about him last year. But right now, it hurts to be near him. I wish I were anywhere else.

You did this to yourself, I remind myself. *This was your big master plan.*

It doesn't help. I sigh, open up a document, and begin to type.

* * *

"Miss Jennings. Come here, please."

For the second class in a row, he singles me out. Makes me stay behind. I glance around, sure that someone must find this suspicious, but no one even looks over.

I sigh and step up to the lectern.

"Yes, professor?" I'm not rude. I'm *never* rude. But I make my question as flat as possible. So he knows I've learned my lesson; that I'm no longer eager for his attention.

Far from it. I wish my cap had done its job.

A muscle tics in his jaw. Professor Kent flicks a glance at me, eyes narrowed.

"Next class, please keep your social life out of the lecture hall." The words are dragged out of him. Reluctant and heavy.

"I... what?"

I don't understand. I have friends, sure, but they're not in this class.

"Your *friend*—" he spits the word "—barely wrote a single note. Was too busy drooling all over your bare legs. If you're going to distract the other students—"

"Hang on." I hold up a palm. "So the guy next to me didn't pay attention. How is that *my* fault?"

He keeps talking like I never spoke. "—Then I will be forced to introduce a seating plan."

I snort. I can't help it. This whole situation is so ridiculous. He's mad that some random guy didn't listen properly, and somehow I'm to blame? And the big threat is a seating plan—like I'm supposed to care?

"Fine." I shrug. "You're the professor. You can do whatever stupid thing you want."

I'm being outright rude now, but he started this whole mess. And if I stay here one more minute, I'll do something worse. Like grab a fistful of his perfect, pressed shirt and *shake* him. Like let slip how badly his words hurt.

"Avery." He says it like a warning. I turn on my heel, ready to leave.

Professor Kent catches my elbow again, just like last time. Only this time, he doesn't drop me like he's been burned. This time, he tugs me to a stop, his grip warm and firm.

His hand is on my bare skin. A shiver runs through me, from the crown of my head to my toes.

I ignore it, scowling at him over my shoulder. "I tried to transfer like you said. I sat at the back and kept my distance. *You're* the one making this harder, professor."

He inhales sharply, nostrils flaring. He still hasn't dropped my arm.

"I know, Avery." His thumb rubs a tiny circle onto my skin.

Like he can't help it. "You're right. I know. I'm handling this all wrong."

I didn't expect that. His confession takes me by surprise, makes my lips part as I stare up at him. He's so much taller than me, and I only really feel it when he's close. When he has me in arm's reach, towering against my back. His gray eyes are stormy, his dark hair curling over his forehead, and how the hell does anyone concentrate when he's around? My heart patters against my rib cage, like it's knocking to get out.

I wet my lip.

"*Avery.*"

"I won't," I promise, though I don't really know what he's afraid of. I tug my arm gently out of his grip and back up two steps. "I'm not trying to cause you trouble," I tell him quietly. And I don't know what comes over me, but I say the rest too. "I just… missed you. I wanted you near."

Something dark flickers across his face. He opens his mouth to say something, but I pound down the steps and out of the lecture hall before I have to hear it.

I know he doesn't want me. I know I got it all wrong.

But I can't hear it from him.

I can't.

Ellis

⚭

Distance. That's what I needed. Some space from the way Avery nibbles on her plump bottom lip when she's thinking. A reprieve from her cherry scent wafting past me in the corridors. Two weeks into the semester, and I've barely looked in her direction. Barely heard her voice at all.

I feel better already.

That's what I tell myself, anyway, as I lean back in my office chair, scrubbing my face and groaning at the ceiling. It's late to still be on campus. The evening sky is bruised, the light fading, and outside my office window, campus is almost empty. The old-fashioned street lamps that dot the sidewalks flicker on one by one, and I stare outside without really seeing anything.

Who am I kidding? She doesn't have to be near. She doesn't even have to be within a ten mile radius.

Everywhere I look, I see Avery.

Every sound I hear reminds me of her. Her soft footsteps over the floorboards; the whisper of her hair over her bare shoulders; the hitch in her breath when she laughs silently at a joke in her head.

I could never look in her direction again and she'd still be imprinted on my mind. Would still be the face I see when I go to sleep.

Avery Jennings.

Fuck.

How is she doing? Does she like her other classes? Does she like *my* class, or have I ruined it for her?

All questions that I can't seek the answers for.

"God help me." This is what it's come to: talking to myself in my office at night. I stifle a laugh, rolling my head on my neck.

"Professor Kent?" Her knock is so quiet, her knuckles just brushing the door. For a crazy second, I think I've done it. I've finally gone mad; pined for Avery so badly that I've started hallucinating her. But when I glance at the doorway, expecting only shadows, there she is. Hovering anxiously on the threshold, fiddling with her hair.

"Avery?"

Did I make this happen somehow? Did I email her, summon her here, then conveniently forget about it, wiping my memory with shame?

"Hi." We're alone, the English building empty for hours now, so her whisper comes out louder than it usually does. It echoes across my silent office, undeniable. "I, um." She coughs quietly. Her hand twitches. "I have a question about the assignment."

Disappointment roars up in me, sudden and overwhelming. It's crushing and violent; it squashes the air from my chest.

I force a smile. Gesture to the chair opposite.

"Of course. How can I help, Miss Jennings?"

"Avery." Her cheeks pink as she crosses to the chair. Her cut off shorts rustle as she walks. "Please don't go backward. You called me Avery before." She settles down, always so delicate. Her ankles cross below her seat, her legs smooth and bare and tanned from the summer, and when she inhales sharply, I tear my eyes back to her face.

"Excuse me." I don't know which part I'm apologizing for. *All* of it, I guess. "How can I help, Avery?"

Her mouth twitches in a shy smile. "That's better."

A reluctant grin cracks my cheeks. The moment stretches between us, taut and thrumming; there's no sound except for our shared breaths and the breeze tickling the window. Her eyes are so wide, so blue, and I couldn't look away if I tried.

So I don't try. And heat blooms under my skin, my body warming up for something that can't happen.

"So." I clear my throat. "The assignment?"

"Right." Avery ducks her head, the flush deepening on her cheeks. I want to round this desk, crouch in front of her chair, and cradle her face. I want to kiss her forehead and tell her not to be embarrassed. "I just, um. I picked Macbeth for the essay. And I—"

"Not Romeo and Juliet?" I tilt my head, watching her closely. Her breath catches in one of her silent laughs, the corner of her mouth tugging up. She sees the irony too.

"No. I don't like that one, professor."

"Why not?" I'm drawing her off topic, but I can't help it. Avery Jennings seems like exactly the sort of girl who'd love Romeo and Juliet. She paints her nails a pretty pearl color; she takes time weaving elaborate braids through her hair. Last year, when she took my class, I came to the lecture hall early a few times and found her reading romance novels.

It was so fucking cute. I could barely tear my eyes off her.

Avery shrugs one shoulder. "There's no one reason. I mean, the misunderstandings are pretty dumb. And the family feud thing is so unnecessary. But I guess the real thing is that I prefer happy endings."

I lean forward, bracing my elbows on my desk. Clasp my hands and watch her over the top of my knuckles. "Macbeth isn't exactly a fairy tale."

Avery smiles at me properly then, her wicked streak flashing through.

"Maybe not. But you can't deny that he really loved his wife."

I tip my head back and laugh, the sound bouncing off the ceiling. When was the last time I laughed—*really* laughed? It feels alien, out of practice, and I'm immediately lighter. Like I've shaken something loose.

"You're right, as usual." Avery bites her lip, pleased, as I grab a spare sheet of paper. "Let's go through the assignment."

If someone had asked me two weeks ago whether I could sit—alone—in my office after hours with Avery Jennings and not make a huge mistake, I'd have told them no. That she's too much of a temptation. My shy, blonde kryptonite.

But here I am, doing my job. Acting like the professor I'm supposed to be. We go through her assignment plan, point by point, and I don't even look at her bare legs again. We keep it professional, on topic, and if I have to stop breathing through my nose halfway through because her cherry scent addles my senses—well.

It's adapt or die.

"Does that help?" I ask at last, leaning back in my chair. I'm grateful for every spare inch between us. She flips her hair over one shoulder, fiddling with the ends absentmindedly, and I fist my hands beneath the desk to keep from reaching for her.

"Yes. Thank you. Um."

We're done. I made it. I kept my messed up desires for my student to myself. Yet she's still sitting there, blinking at me wide-eyed, and I peer around my office like an idiot.

"Was there something else?"

Avery nods and stands up. Balls her hands into fists. Fixes her gaze on a spot on the wall just above my head.

"I-wish-you-would-look-at-me-again." She says it so fast, the words jumbling together, that it takes me a second to work out what she said. Then I frown at her, my heart thumping harder in my chest.

"I'm looking at you now."

"No." She swallows. "In class."

"I *can't* look at you in class, Avery."

"Why not—"

"Because everyone will see!" I'm talking way too loud, my voice bouncing around my silent office. Anyone walking through the shadowed corridors; anyone wandering past the window—they'll hear it all. But the words burst out of me, desperate and vicious, because how can she not see this? How does she not understand? "I'll take one look at you and every fucker in that room will know how I feel about you, Avery. I—I can't—"

I break off, chest heaving, staring blindly out the window. She's holding her breath, she's so quiet, but then the floorboards creak as she shifts her weight.

"How *do* you feel about me?"

"Avery." I tear my gaze away from the window. Level her a look. "You *know*. You've always known."

I'm right. I know I am, and Avery confirms it with her shaky

24

inhale. She nods once—a truce. And when she grabs her bag and crosses to the doorway, I don't know if I'm more frustrated or relieved.

She turns on the threshold. "Thanks for your help, Professor Kent."

"You're welcome." A thought occurs to me, and I frown. "You're not walking home alone in the dark, are you?"

"No." She smiles at me softly. "I'm meeting my friend Paige." She taps lightly on the door frame. "Why? Would you have walked me home?"

"Yes. I would."

It's a confession. Because though that may sound noble, we both know what it means. What would inevitably happen at the end of that walk, when the last of my control ebbed away.

"Goodnight, Professor Kent."

"Goodnight, Avery."

I wait until her footsteps fade down the corridor. Then I dig the heels of my palms into my eyes, like I can gouge her gorgeous image right out of them.

Avery

❧

I know it's wrong to think sinful thoughts about my professor. And I know it's wrong to—to *torment* him with how badly I want him. But I've been dreaming of him for nearly a year now. Touching myself, imagining his hands. Picking my clothes to match his favorite colors. I just can't help it.

When he stands at the lectern, so broody and commanding, shivers ripple over my skin. My mouth gets drier the longer I look at him, and there's this pulsing ache between my legs. His low, clear voice vibrates right through to my bones.

In the third week of the semester, I don't wear a bra to class. It's not *obvious*. I'm wearing a loose, draping sweater. No one else even bats an eye. But when I'm sitting five rows back, legs crossed and thighs squeezing, I feel the exact moment that Professor Kent's gaze snags on my chest.

The way he looks at me—it's always a caress. A lingering physical touch from across the room. But this time, his eyes lock on the front of my sweater, and my nipples bead and push against the fabric. The more he stares, the tighter they become, until I'm breathless, squirming in the row with my pen gripped between my knuckles.

"The themes…" He catches himself. Shakes his head. Carries on, his voice hoarse. "The dominant themes in Shakespeare's plays…"

I don't listen. Lord, I'm awful, but I just can't concentrate when Professor Kent is standing right in front of me. Every day after class, I go home and look up the slides. Read them over and try to take the lesson in this time.

Sometimes I touch myself too. Remembering his deep voice washing over me.

"Miss Jennings."

I'm not surprised this time, when he calls me aside at the end of the lecture. I hop up onto the platform, hiding a smile, and wait for everyone to leave with my ankles crossed. I play with my hair, because I know he likes that. It always makes his eyes darken.

"Your clothing…" As soon as the door bangs shut, the sound bouncing around the hall, he begins to speak. His gray eyes dart to me and away. Professor Kent grips the lectern, unmoving even though everyone's gone. Like this lump of old wood is the only thing anchoring him in place.

"What about it?" I murmur when he stalls. It's not like the professor to hold back.

But he drops his head, gusting out a sigh that's dredged from the bottom of his soul.

"Avery," he says to the lectern. "Are you trying to kill me?"

I huff a laugh. Is it that obvious?

"Kill you? No, that's not it."

He risks a glance at me, staring when he finds my soft smile. I know I've done wrong. I know he's mad. But I'm so freaking happy to be alone with him again. When it's just the two of us, talking together, standing close enough to share breaths—something untangles on my insides.

"Then what *are* you doing?"

I wet my lip. "I told you before, in your office. I want you to look at me again."

"But—"

"I miss you when you don't." I shrug one shoulder, abruptly shy. Like so many things when it comes to Professor Kent, I didn't think this through. "Sorry," I whisper. "I won't do it again."

"That's probably for the best," he rasps, gaze dropping to my chest again. And I can't help it. I arch my back the tiniest bit. I push the tight beads of my nipples harder against the fabric. They're so sensitive, the brush of my soft sweater makes my breath catch.

"Avery." Professor Kent rubs a hand over his jaw, still staring. "You're making a devil out of me."

"You can touch them." I don't know where this is coming from. There was nothing like this in my self help manuals. All I know is that feeling his gaze on me—it's *right*. It's decadent. Like sliding into a warm bath after a long day. And I'd say just about anything to keep him looking. For him to touch me, to *taste* me…

Oh god. I clench my thighs tighter.

"We can't." His chest is heaving. He turns to me, even as he says no. Takes a step away from the lectern. "I'm your professor, Avery. You're a student. This is wrong."

"It doesn't feel wrong." I wrap my arms around my waist and hug myself. Even though I know he's being reasonable, that he's doing the right thing, somehow that *hurts*. It's another rejection to add to the pile. "How can it be wrong when I l-love you—"

"Avery." His voice whip-cracks through the quiet. "Don't. Don't say things like that."

My eyes blur. His face swims in front of me, his pale jaw and his wavy dark hair going all smudgy. I blink hard, a hot tear rolling down my cheek.

"God. No, Avery…" He sounds broken.

Well, that makes two of us. I wrap my arms tighter around my waist, holding myself together by the seams. And I wish I had a great parting line. Something for him to dwell over. But the truth is, my tongue is glued to the roof of my mouth. I couldn't speak if I tried.

My chin wobbles in the most humiliating way, and all I can do is nod, give a pathetic little squeak, and scurry to the door. My bag thumps against my hip, my sandals skid over the floorboards, and god, I'm such a mess.

One of these days, I'll learn my lesson. I'll stop laying my heart bare for this man. Stop throwing myself at his feet like I'm sacrificing myself at an altar.

One of these days, I will *learn*.

After all: Professor Kent is an excellent teacher.

Ellis

I am not a reckless man, especially where Avery Jennings is concerned. Everything I do, I do with utmost control. With an iron clad restraint that chafes at my insides, that makes my heart twist.

Because with Avery, I have no other choice. And I refuse to hurt her. To make her life harder; to ruin her college experience.

Except… that's exactly what I've done. In my determination to keep her at arm's length so that she can be a normal, happy student—I've *hurt* her.

I made Avery Jennings cry.

I've never felt so fucking small. My chest cracks open at the sight of that single tear, trembling against her eyelashes before it falls. She sucks in a wobbly breath, lip quivering, then high-tails it out of the lecture hall like I'm someone to *run* from.

No. No, no, no. This is—this is *exactly* what I was trying to avoid. Avery, eyes wide, blinking hard in pain at my words.

Avery, fleeing from my presence with her arms wrapped around her middle. Everything else falls away but her.

I need to go to her. Soothe her.

So when I set my jaw and stride out of the lecture hall, I don't care who sees. I don't care if the students thronging the corridor blink at me, surprised by the shadows clouding my face. I don't care if other professors glance at me, do a double take, then mutter to each other in concern.

I stride after Avery like an avenging angel. My sweet girl will *not* cry another tear because of me.

Her blonde head bobs through the crowd ahead of me. She's rushing, tripping on the grass in her haste. Bouncing off the footballers' shoulders as they swagger to class.

I follow. Steady but sure. She won't slip out of my sight again.

Someone speaks to me, addressing me by name. Asks about next week's reading. I ignore them, pushing past, their voice little more to me than the birds singing in the trees.

I need to get to Avery.

She darts off the busy path, ducking inside the library side entrance. The hem of that goddamn floaty sweater whips through the door behind her. I step onto the grass, cutting a line straight after her, and when I push inside the library, the sudden gloom blinds my eyes.

It's dim in here. Stacks loom high on either side, crammed with books about some obscure subject. Far off in the room, there's the scratch of pens. The tapping of keys. But this section—it's like another world. Shadowed and silent, tinted blue. Like it's underwater.

"Avery."

She's huddled against a bookcase, leaning one shoulder on

the shelf. Her head is ducked, shoulders heaving, but she whips around when I say her name. Her gasp shatters the silence.

"P-professor…"

"Come with me."

I don't give her a chance to argue. I take her by the elbow, gentle but firm, and guide her between the bookshelves to a more private spot. Not for me, not to protect my career, but because Avery is vulnerable. Wet-faced and whimpering. When I've made sure we're alone, I take her by the shoulders. Brace her against the stacks, rubbing small circles against the fabric of her thin sweater.

"Avery. Sweet girl. Tell me why you're crying."

She hiccups in outrage. And I stifle a smile as she hisses, "Why do you *think?*"

That's my girl. She's shy, yes, but beneath those blushes and whispers, she has a steel core. And she won't put up with bullshit.

"I don't know," I tell her. She puffs up, ready to bite my head off, but I keep talking in a low murmur. "It can't be because I told you off for your clothing." I fix her a look. Let a ragged sigh gust out of me as I glance at her chest again. Despite her tears, her nipples are still pebbled against the fabric. Little bullets, headed straight for my heart. "Because you wanted to torture me with this flimsy sweater. Didn't you?"

Avery gulps. Sniffles again. And I do what I've been burning to do since I first saw her this morning: I take one hand off her shoulder and hover it over her breast. A hair's breadth from the gorgeous swell, just crying out for my hands, my lips, my *teeth*.

"Do you still want me to touch them, Avery?"

She scowls up at me, a tiny line creasing her forehead. But

then she presses her mouth together and nods. I groan and step forward, flattening her against the stacks, and her surprised gasp fills me with heat.

"What?" I rock against her without thinking. Every urge I've tamped down over the last year, every impulse I've tamed—they all rush back in full force. Take over my thrumming body, my desperate hands, my hard voice. "You think I can touch your gorgeous tits and not the rest of you? You think I can walk away with barely a taste?" I press my mouth against her temple, teeth bared, and feel her pulse hammering against the delicate skin.

Her hips tilt up, thrusting against mine, and it's almost enough to make me blow here and now.

Her fingers wind in my shirt. Clutch at the fabric. "I'm still mad at you," she mumbles, her head tipping back on a moan as I lick at her throat.

"I know." I knead the mound of her breast, pinching her nipple, savoring her ragged groan. Bury my other hand in her soft, wild hair fraying out of its braid. "Because you think I don't love you." I punctuate my words with a rock of my hips. "You. Think. You. Don't. *Own*. Me."

"I... I..." Avery's gone. Blissed out and bemused, her eyes staring glassy at the ceiling. So I tear my hands away from her. Step back, even though every molecule in me screams out to flatten her against the shelves, to kiss and fuck and claim.

I won't do it when she's upset. When she's not thinking clearly. Even though my cock's so hard, my teeth ache.

"You're a smart girl, Avery." I scrub a hand over my jaw, chest heaving. And I look at her, *really* look at her, with every ounce of my need for her written on my face. She whimpers, pupils blowing wide, and reaches for me.

I back up another step.

"Don't make this mistake again," I rasp. "Don't you dare forget what this is."

She nods, dazed, her eyes finally dry. And though my hand itches to wipe away the old tears on her cheeks, I don't trust myself. If I touch her again, I'll be buried in her sweet pussy before I can think straight.

I turn on my heel and leave her there, her cherry scent lingering on my clothes.

* * *

I make it home. That's my only saving grace in this car wreck of a situation. I wait until I'm safely tucked away in my apartment before I tear my buckle open, panting hard between my clenched teeth. I lean against my front door, shoulder blades digging into the wood, and *punish* myself, fast and hard.

I can't go slow. Or gentle. Or touch myself in any way that Avery would. I can't picture her small, soft hand wrapped around my length. Better to grip myself hard enough to bruise, choking my cock, and push myself to a painful orgasm, quick and rough.

When I'm done, my head thumps back against the door. My hoarse breaths fill my silent apartment. I screw my eyes shut, and for the millionth time, I picture her *here.* In my home.

Curled up on my sofa, painting her nails. Sipping hot chocolate and watching a movie. Puttering around in the kitchen, already knowing where everything is. Eating food from my refrigerator, sleeping in my bed, stepping into my shower.

Living here, always in reach.

Her soft skin moments away from my touch. Her cherry scent lacing the air. I can picture it now, so vividly that my chest aches; I can almost taste her on my tongue.

I haven't kissed her. Not on the lips. I haven't crossed that line.

It's just as well. If I had, I'd never have been able to leave her there.

I used to like this place. But it hasn't been *home* since that first day that Avery sat in my class. Since I laid eyes on her and the earth cracked open beneath my feet. Now my apartment is cold. Quiet. Mocking me, in its lack of her.

One day, I think, sudden and fierce. I won't pursue her now. Won't do more damage than I already have. But the second being with me wouldn't hurt her, wouldn't cause her trouble...

Avery Jennings will never want to leave. I'll make sure of that, hosting her like a gentleman. Burying my face between her thighs every chance I get. And if she wants to live somewhere else—wants to travel? Work abroad?

I don't care. Wherever she is, I'll be there too.

Avery

"He *what?*"

Paige gapes at me from the other end of the sofa, a piece of popcorn hovering halfway to her mouth. Her caramel hair is scraped back in a bun, and she's still dressed in her leotard and sweatpants.

Leona sits on the rug, her back leaning against the sofa. A sketchpad is balanced on her knees, with charcoal staining the tips of her fingers and forming a streak over one cheek. She snorts.

"Come on, Paige. He kissed her."

I pace back and forth in front of the TV. A sitcom is paused on the screen, the characters frozen and flickering in place.

"No, he didn't. Not exactly. I mean, his lips didn't touch my lips."

"But?" Leona prods. She's hiding a smirk as she watches me, eyes sparkling. Leona acts tough, but she's loves romance just as much as the rest of us.

"But he might as well have." I sigh, dropping my satchel onto the floorboards. I close my eyes and summon the feelings from the library—every single sensation. Professor Kent plastering me to the bookcase, touching me, rubbing his face in my hair. Speaking with his mouth pressed to my temple, like he couldn't bear to lean back an inch.

Maybe he didn't kiss me. But he sure did stake a claim.

"He told me he loves me." I swirl a finger in the air. I open my eyes and find Paige beaming. "In a roundabout way."

"That's the dream," Leona says flatly, but I ignore her. She's just worried about me. She's spent a lot of nights sat up with me lately, rubbing my back as I sniffle about Professor Kent.

"But he won't be with me." My shoulders slump as the rest of our encounter crashes back in. The way he tore himself off, gritting his teeth like it hurt. The way he stared at me with hungry eyes, before inhaling sharply and striding away.

"Because of his career?" Paige finally remembers her popcorn, dropping it back in the bowl in her lap.

"No…" I chew on my bottom lip. "I don't think that's it. I think he's—he's protecting me."

Leona rolls her eyes. Paige shudders out a huge sigh.

"Oh, *wow*. That is so romantic."

I prop my hands on my hips. Stare at the floorboards. "It *is* romantic. But it has to stop. If he doesn't want to be with me…" I suck in a painful breath. "Then, okay. That's one thing. I'll accept it. But if he *does* want to be with me, and he's making my decision for me—"

"He'd better cut it out," Leona finishes. I point at her.

"Right."

"We need a plan." Leona tosses her sketchpad onto the coffee table and rolls her head from side to side. Nerves swell in my belly, fluttering against my insides, but I blow out a hard breath and nod.

She's right. I need a plan.

A plan to break Professor Kent.

* * *

I wait until his office hours the next day. A whole agonizing day of lectures and classes on campus; of knowing that he's near and feeling his touch still tingling on my skin, but not going to him.

Not yet.

At 5pm, when my last class ends and his office hours begin, I meet Leona and Paige in the girls' bathroom in the English building. The door has barely swung shut behind me before they tug me to the sinks, patting at my hair and fussing over my makeup.

We already picked out my outfit last night: a white halter dress and sandals. But now, in the safety of the girls' bathroom, Leona adds the finishing touches to her master plan.

Paige brushes my hair and fluffs it up until it rests lightly on my shoulders. Leona reaches over and dabs red lipstick on my mouth—bold and bright. Then squirts perfume on my chest.

And I slide a hand up my back and flick my bra open. It's time to pull out all the stops.

* * *

His door is propped open. I pause on the threshold, watching Professor Kent in his office. He's sat at the desk, a pair of black-framed glasses balanced on his nose, and a muscle flexes in his jaw as he reads over some poor student's assignment.

He gusts out a low sigh, grabbing a pen and crossing through a whole section with a firm line.

I clear my throat. God, I hope that's not my paper.

Professor Kent glances over, then does a double take. His eyes widen, and he drops the pen quickly, pushing to his feet.

"Avery. What are you—"

"These are your office hours, right?" He presses his mouth in a line and nods. Here goes nothing. "I have some questions for you."

Something like disappointment flickers behind his eyes, but the professor waves at the chair opposite his desk. I push off the door, tugging it shut behind me.

"Avery," he warns as he sits back down. His alarm only grows when he gets a good look at me. My hair; my red lips; my nipples beading against my white dress. He hisses out a breath, falling back in his seat. Professor Kent scrubs a hand over his jaw, staring at me with hard, hungry eyes.

"What did you want to ask me?" he rasps.

I reach the spare chair. Grip it, and tug it to one side.

"I'll show you," I whisper.

My summer of self help manuals has been leading to this: the exact moment when I drop to my knees. I crawl under the wood of his desk, shadowed but spacious, as Professor Kent curses darkly above me. He shoves his chair back, spreading his thighs to make room.

I crawl between those legs, resting my palms on his tense muscles.

"Avery." He stares down at me from above the desk, white-faced, his chest heaving. "We can't do this." But even as he says it, he winds his fingers through my hair. Cradles my head like I'm something precious.

I glance pointedly at the hard line straining against his pants. "If we want to, we can."

He chokes out a laugh. He's so tense, his thighs are practically vibrating. I bite my lip, waiting until he meets my eyes.

"Please." I dart my tongue out to wet my lip. Professor Kent *groans.* "Please, professor. I want to taste you."

"Fuck." He runs the pad of one thumb over my red lip. Pushes it inside my mouth, sucking in a ragged breath as I suckle at him, humming. Heat tingles under my skin, my core pulsing under my dress, and I wiggle my hips from side to side, so worked up I need to *move.*

He's so close. So solid and manly. His thumb is large in my mouth, and his manhood would be so much larger. His scent is everywhere, surrounding me, and I'm tucked down here in the shadows like his dirty little secret.

I love it.

"Avery." He sounds broken already. Power surges through me, heady and delicious, as he pumps his thumb back and forth on my tongue. "God, sweetheart. That dress. Those lips. You look…"

I pull off his thumb with a *pop.* Tilt my head.

"I look?"

He says it quietly. Confesses it, just for me.

"Like one of my daydreams."

That's all I need to hear. He wants me, wants this too, and to demonstrate, he helps me get his pants open. I reach in, biting my lip, and have to stifle a moan when I finally get my hand around him.

He's scorching hot. Rock hard, the skin like satin. With a bead of moisture crowning the tip. I swirl a fingertip through that bead, spreading the moisture around, and he tips his head back with a groan.

God. The sounds he makes—they're so deep and rumbling, they might shake apart the furniture.

"Professor Kent—"

"Ellis," he interrupts. A rueful smile tugs his mouth, and he strokes my cheekbone. "Call me Ellis."

"Ellis." I looked up his name ages ago. When I first sat in his class last year and blinked up at him like a thunderbolt had hit me. But I'd somehow never dreamed that *I* could call him that.

I love it. His name slips out of me like a sigh.

"I don't know what I'm doing," I admit. I squeeze his hard length gently, running my hand up and down. "You might have to teach me a bit longer, professor."

"Fuck." He shakes his head, dazed. "Fuck. I'm going to hell."

I sit back on my heels, heart sinking. "Do you want to stop?"

"No." The growl tears out of him, thrilling me back to life. I push back onto my knees and squeeze him again. "God, no. I'm going to feel your pretty mouth. Start now, sweetheart. Taste the tip."

He slips back into his role of teacher easily. And pleasure crackles through my veins as he takes charge, always so steady and sure. He's as firm as ever, his words commanding, and I pant and squeeze my thighs together as I do what he says.

He tastes *good.* Salty and subtle. I moan and suck him into my mouth without being told. Ellis curses and tightens his grip in my hair, guiding me up and down beneath the desk.

"That's it." I bob my head, my lips stretching around him. "That's right, sweetheart. Swallow me down. Taste it. It's all yours." I hum, the vibration soaking through his skin, and he hisses between his teeth. Rocks his hips up to meet me, his desk chair creaking.

Yes. I may be on my knees, may have my mouth on him, but I've never felt so powerful. Never felt so certain and in control. I was made to do this—to draw these sounds from this man, and to feel his hands on me in turn.

Muffled footsteps by the door. That's our only warning. Ellis pushes his chair beneath the desk, hiding his lap, and I scramble to tuck my feet under.

The office door swings open. An older woman's voice floats through the room, asking Ellis about his class schedule.

I hold my breath, heart slamming in my throat. I don't dare move. Don't dare creak the floorboards. From here to the doorway, I'm hidden by the desk. But if she steps inside...

Ellis answers, polite and unruffled.

I bite my lip, suddenly desperate to laugh. And to do the most wicked thing I can think of. I take his length in my hand, still hard and flushed angry red, and slide it back into my mouth.

Ellis' breath catches. See, he's not so unflappable, is he? And when he keeps chatting with the woman, his voice is ever so slightly strained. I smile around his cock, bobbing my head slowly. Sucking him quietly; savoring every lick and taste. One of his knees is pressed close to me, and I rub my beaded nipple on his leg through the fabric of my dress.

The woman says something.

"Thanks, Elaine," Ellis grits out. And when his office door clicks shut, footsteps moving away down the corridor, he curses roughly and pushes his chair back. I crawl after him eagerly, my mouth still on his cock, dipping my head with every nudge of his hand. He guides me faster and faster, his hand gripped in my hair, and the extra roughness makes my body sing.

"Shit. You liked that, didn't you? Sweet little exhibitionist. Did you want her to catch you under there, with your lips around my cock and your pussy soaking through the back of your dress?"

I hum and nod, taking him deeper, and he curses one more time before gritting out, "Avery. Going to come."

That's my warning. I know *that* much. My cue to pull away if I don't want to swallow. But I *do* want to—I want all of him. Every last drop.

So I crowd closer, taking him so deep that my nose touches his stomach.

"Avery." I'll never get tired of him saying my name like that. Like a prayer. Like something holy. "Sweetheart. Fuck." He comes long and hard, his hips thrusting off his chair. And when I finally sit back on my heels, wiping my hand over my mouth, I don't have time to catch my breath before he's bundling me out from under the desk.

He scoops me up off the floorboards, sets me on the desk, and tears my panties down my legs.

"Yes?" He pauses with my thighs pushed wide apart. He's got such a crazed glint in his eye, I think he'd go mad if I said no.

I wet my lip, suddenly shy. "Yes, please, professor."

Ellis groans as he drops to his knees. Buries his face between my thighs and *eats* at me like a starving man. I'm already wound so tight from squirming under the desk, and feeling his tongue plunge inside my entrance, feeling his teeth scrape over my clit—

I fall apart.

I come with a wail, my thighs locked around his neck, and

he doesn't stop for a second. Doesn't ease off until I slump over his papers, boneless.

And when we finally both get back up, clumsy with pleasure, he laughs, the sound bright, and kisses my mouth. So sweet, so tender, but claiming, too. That's Professor Kent all over: soft hands and nipping teeth.

Ten minutes later, I jump when I let myself out of his office and find someone waiting in the corridor. It's the guy who sat next to me on the first day of class. Who kept staring at me instead of taking notes. A knot tightens in my stomach, nerves skittering over my skin, but he doesn't smile knowingly. Doesn't make any hint that he heard us. Just tips his chin and says, "Hey."

"Hi." I hurry away, thanking my lucky stars.

That was super close.

Ellis

❧

I stride into the lecture hall ten minutes before class begins. Usually, I prefer to arrive precisely on time. Better than standing at the lectern with sleepy students gawking.

But I was too eager this morning. I need to see her.

Avery slips through the doorway two minutes later, her cheeks flushed and her eyes bright. She's wearing a pair of cut off shorts and a loose, light sweater today, but no matter how demure she looks, my cock swells in my pants.

I've seen her gasping. Squirming. Calling out my name.

I'll never be able to look at her without my pulse pounding again.

"Hi, professor," she whispers, smiling shyly before she crosses to climb the steps. I stare, fixated on her bare legs, until someone coughs out a laugh.

Shit. *Get it together.*

I keep my eyes firmly away from Avery as I set up my notes. Prepare for the lecture. And perhaps I would have made it through the full hour, if it weren't for the note which slithers out of my briefcase.

It's handwritten. Torn hastily from a notebook.

I know what you did.

I read it twice, heart thundering. There's only one thing in my life that's worthy of blackmail.

Avery.

My eyes dart to her, helpless, as rage swells in my throat. Whoever sent this note… they'll wish they minded their own goddamn business. Because I don't give a shit about my career—it's Avery I care about. And if they dare to cause her any trouble…

I roll my head from side to side, blowing out a slow breath.

"Problem, professor?"

It's a guy in the third row. He hunches over his desk, watching me eagerly. I blink at him, recognition dawning—it's the guy who came to my office hours. The guy who sat next to Avery and drooled all over her bare legs.

This fucker. I fix him with a hard glare, saying nothing.

He waits a beat too long until his cocky smile slips. Until he registers the violence and fury in my gaze. Then he shrinks back into the row, fumbling for his laptop.

"Never mind," he mutters, throat bobbing.

Goddamn right. *Never mind.*

It's dealt with. This weasel won't dare bother her—it's clear from his ducked head and his darting eyes. He picked a fight without thinking, and now he's running with his tail between his legs. And now he knows that he even so much as *sniffs* Avery—he'll have me to deal with.

Good. Fine.

So why is my heart still racing? Pounding out a sickly rhythm in my chest?

I make it through the lecture. God knows how. I switch onto autopilot, delivering the class that I've given so many times, I could do it in my sleep. And this time, I don't stare at Avery like a love struck fool. No; I keep my frown fixed on the asshole in the third row. He wilts into his chair, penitent and piss-scared, but it doesn't calm my pulse. Doesn't stop the ringing in my ears.

"Are you okay?" Avery whispers at the end of the lecture, when everyone else is filing out, oblivious. Our little blackmailer made a run for it first, his sneakers squeaking over the floorboards.

Avery hops on to the platform, her arms crossed and forehead creased. She's *worried* for me, sweet girl.

"Yes," I grind out, shoving my papers into my briefcase. I know what I have to do. "But last night... Avery, it was a mistake."

Her pained breath reaches my ears. *Finally* cuts through the chaos in my head. And as soon as I hear it, I know—what the hell am I doing?

"You—you *asshole*." She wraps her arms around her waist tighter. Hugging, because I've hurt her so badly.

"Avery. Wait." She turns on her heel. I catch her by the elbow, chest thundering and breath coming fast. "*Wait.* I'm sorry. That's not—I don't think that."

"You don't know *what* you think," she says coldly, and god, I've never heard that tone from her. It chills me down to my marrow.

"I do." I spin her back to face me. Cradle her cheek. She glares up at me, eyes hard. "I know that I love you. That I can't spend another day without you. Sneaking around, like this is something to be ashamed of." Her frown softens as I talk,

47

melting into something cautious. Something hopeful. "I know I've messed up so many times. And you're such an angel, I'll never deserve you. But please, Avery." I drop my forehead to hers. Skate my thumbs over her cheekbones. "Be with me. Be mine."

She bites her bottom lip. Draws in a steady breath. Then *smiles,* and it's like the sun coming out.

"I love you too." She falters, glancing at the door. The noise of the crowd echoes in from the corridor. "What about your job?"

"There are other jobs." I scoop her up by the ass. Carry her down off the platform and sit her down on the front row of desks, her legs wrapped around my waist. "There's only one Avery Jennings."

It's nothing like last night. Even with the thunder of footsteps in the corridor, the shouts of students so near, we're not frantic. We take our time.

I kiss Avery like I should have kissed her in the library. Slow and sweet and thorough. And she undoes my belt almost lazily, drawing the leather through the buckle.

Still. When I slide my hand inside her shorts, my fingers delving into her panties, she's wet. Slick and ready. I drop my forehead onto her shoulder, forcing myself to think straight.

"Someone might come in," I rasp. "Do you want to stop?"

"No." She tugs me closer by the belt loops. Spreads her legs wider. "I want you to take me, professor."

"I fucking knew it," I mutter, yanking her shorts and panties down. Pushing home into her tight, warm pussy. She tenses at the intrusion, and I slow, her breaths hot on my neck. But after a few seconds, she relaxes. Starts humming and nibbling my earlobe. And I slide in to the hilt.

"You're my sweet little exhibitionist, aren't you?" She nods, hiccuping when I spank her ass. I start to rock my hips, her stranglehold on my cock making sweat bead on my forehead. So. Goddamn. Good. "And you're *mine*. All mine, Avery. Mine to fuck. Mine to love. Mine to marry."

She whimpers, clinging to my shoulders as I pound between her legs. As I reach between us and play with her clit. The sounds of the corridor are loud, deafening all around us, but we might as well be the last two people on Earth. The row shudders beneath us, scraping over the floorboards, but I don't stop. I thrust harder, faster.

"You're mine, too," she whispers in my ear. Squeezes her little pussy to make her point. And that's what breaks me—what makes my vision go white. I groan, rubbing her clit and cursing with relief when she comes, clamping down hard on me, waves of pleasure wracking her body.

I fill her up. Pulse after pulse. So much that it drips onto the desk.

I don't care. I'll clean it up. Or maybe I'll leave it there for the next nosy asshole.

"Don't you dare take this back," Avery says once she's caught her breath. She hops down off the row and tugs her clothes back on.

I choke out a laugh, filled with sunshine. Filled with *her*.

"Never."

It's done. She's *mine*.

Avery

One Year Later

I drift between the library stacks, peering up the spines of endless books. The stack in my arms is already weighing me down. Making my muscles burn.

"Want a hand?"

I turn to tell my would-be savior 'no'. That I've got it, thank you. But when I spin, I find Ellis leaning against the book case, a smirk tugging his mouth.

"Oh my god!" I yelp. Someone shushes me from three stacks over. "Oh my god," I whisper, rolling my eyes. Ellis grins, pushing upright and plucking the pile of books out of my arms. He drops a kiss on my forehead.

"I love it when you call me that."

"Shut up." I trail him between the bookcases. "I thought the conference was until tomorrow morning."

I've been counting the days. Sighing like a war widow. Leona has thrown at least three pens at my head.

50

"I drove back early." Ellis winks at me over his shoulder. "Couldn't keep away."

This is it. The feeling grows in my chest, expanding until I might float up to the ceiling. *This is it.* The man I love. This is the rest of my life.

"I missed you," I murmur, my throat weirdly tight. He glances at me, concerned. And why shouldn't he be? Two seconds ago, we were messing around. Chatting playfully.

Now there's a lump in my throat and tears swim in my eyes.

"Avery." He gathers me against his chest. Tucks my head under his chin. "Sweet girl. I *always* miss you."

It's hard not having him near. Oh, we spend every night together. We see each other every day. But since Ellis took a job at a neighboring college, I can't sneak into his office anymore. Can't peer around for him in the crowds.

"Stupid rules," I mutter. Ellis tips his head back and laughs. Someone shushes us again, but he ignores them, unfazed.

In fact, he backs me up against the bookshelves. Kisses me hard, then nips at my chin.

"You like some rules," he murmurs, his free hand sliding up my waist. Grazing the underside of my breast. "Breaking them, anyway." He places my pile of books on the shelf. Grips both my hips and squeezes tight. "Shall I make you feel better, Avery?"

I nod, grinning blearily at the ceiling as he ducks his head. Licks and nibbles at my neck.

It's hard when he's gone, yes. But he's back now.

And we have the rest of our lives to make up for lost time.

Ellis

Eight Years Later

I never lock my home office door.

For one thing, I have nothing to hide. Teaching college-level English is rewarding, but not exactly top-secret.

For another, my wife likes to visit. Likes to slip inside when I'm working and distract me. Today's outfit is so reminiscent, it makes my chest pinch: a soft white sweater and cherry red lipstick.

"What are you doing?" Avery murmurs, strolling around my desk. Trailing her fingertips over the wood, her ring sparkling up at me. Triumph surges in my gut, the same as every time I see that ring. The proof that she's mine, that it's *my* job to make her happy.

"Nice hair," I tell her, ignoring her question. She's scraped it back into French braids. She knows I like those.

Avery smirks, coming to a stop opposite the desk. She drums her fingers on the polished wood, raising her eyebrows and glancing at the floorboards. There's a cushion ready and waiting for her knees.

A thump rattles the office door. We both jump, startled from the spell we'd begun to weave, then Avery laughs and crosses to the doorway.

"Daddy's working," she whispers to the two giggling boys.

"But you came in," one of them points out, voice high and reedy.

"He has a point," I call.

Avery ignores me, flipping me off behind her back. I grin at the ceiling, leaning back in my chair.

Things have changed. But not the most important things. My wife is still my world, and now our sons have joined us. Made our family bigger and brighter.

I nudge the cushion beneath the desk with my toe, smile rueful.

Maybe next time.

II

Ballet Master

Description

He's a legendary dancer. A man of unmatched skill.

And he won't stop staring at me.

It's a huge opportunity when the famous dancer visits our class. I know that we're lucky, but it sure doesn't feel like that when I keep tripping and missing the music.

I'm just so nervous. A jittery wreck. And every second his eyes stay on me makes it worse.

He doesn't bother watching the rest of the dancers. Only me.

Am I really messing up that badly? Or does the older man with the dark eyes want something else from me...

Something wicked.

Paige

Madame claps her gnarled hands together, an immediate hush settling over the rehearsal studio. She stands in the center of the floor, her back ramrod straight and her chin tilted high. Though she hasn't danced on stage in decades, Madame still holds herself like a prima ballerina. Her graying hair is scraped back into a flawless bun, floaty fabrics flutter around her as she moves, and she watches us along the narrow length of her nose.

"Students."

Her throaty growl comes from her only vice—the cigarettes she still sucks down one after the other at the stage door. A habit from her performing days, when the dancers smoked to settle their nerves and chase the hunger away.

We murmur our greetings. Madame is… unpredictable. Sometimes she shouts that she expects a reply when she speaks. Other times, she wishes silence.

We hedge our bets and murmur quietly. Little indistinct sounds that we can swallow back if she frowns.

"We have a visitor today." She arches one heavily penciled eyebrow. "A very important visitor."

I keep my face carefully blank, my hands clasped loosely in front of my waist. Madame does not tolerate gaudy shows of emotion—it's better to play the silent, dutiful dancer.

Inside, though, curiosity gnaws at my stomach. A visitor? So early in the year?

It's too soon for recruiters from the big dance companies. Too soon for the parade of directors, come to snatch up budding talent.

We haven't even been cast for the showcase yet.

A very important visitor. I fight the urge to fiddle with my worn leotard. If only I'd splashed out last month like I'd planned and bought some new dance clothes.

"You will have heard of Monsieur Dupont."

A sharp intake of breath hisses through the studio. A flash of movement draws my gaze—a man pushing away from the doorway where he was leaning, away from prying eyes. The man strolls into the center of the room to join Madame, a panther's grace in every fluid step.

His dark eyes scan the crowd as we stare at him, shell-shocked.

Raphael Dupont.

The legend.

He's older now than in the videos I've seen—the bootleg clips of his most triumphant performances. The roles he danced that shook the ballet world to its core.

In those clips, he danced with fury, with hunger, with a snarl curling his top lip and sparks glancing from his heels. He was younger then, vibrant and vicious, but the man standing before us still crackles with power. He must be in his late thirties—a retired dancer, yes, but a man in his prime.

"Ladies." Monsieur Dupont nods at the cluster of female dancers in our corner. "Gentlemen." At the men in the other. The faint tinge of his accent has softened since his earlier interviews.

We hold our breath, too afraid to shatter this moment. To risk displeasing this legendary dancer, and carrying that shame for the rest of our lives. The silence hangs in the studio air, taut and shuddering, until Madame claps and the spell is broken.

"Take your places." We hurry to do as she says, lining up at our allocated spots at the barre. "Let's show Monsieur Dupont what you're made of."

What we're made of? I settle a trembling hand on the barre, the polished wood worn smooth by thousands of hands before mine. I'm dressed in a faded gray leotard and there's a tiny ladder at the heel of my pink tights. The satin on the bottom of my pointe shoes is frayed. Wisps of caramel hair frame my face, escaped as always from my bun.

What I'm made of…

I swallow hard, wait for the tinkle of piano keys, and wish I could disappear.

I'm not sure I'm made of anything.

* * *

"Paige."

All around the studio, reflections of me jerk in the mirror. Madame stands at my elbow, watching me run through the warm-up exercises with her mouth pursed.

60

"Yes, Madame?" I murmur, trying not to move my lips. Monsieur Dupont watches us from the front of the room, his arms folded over his broad chest. Even under his long-sleeved black t-shirt, the shift and rise of his sculpted muscles is clear.

Madame starts to say something, then gusts out a sigh. It's not like her to hold back criticism, and I risk glancing in her direction.

Her eyes darken.

"Face forward," she snaps. "Did I tell you to break form?"

"No, Madame."

Monsieur Dupont watches us, his expression tight. Am I messing up so badly? All around us, legs bend and raise. Limbs float through the air, the movement made to look effortless while we sweat and ache and tremble.

"You are wooden." Her harsh words cut through the music. The tips of my ears burn, but I keep dancing. It's so much harder when she is watching me, when *Monsieur Dupont* is watching me, but I try to make my movements fluid. Lyrical.

Perfect.

"Better," she growls, like I've wasted her precious breaths. I don't relax, even when she turns away. She strides across the studio, her heels drumming on the floor, but with the mirrors everywhere, it is never safe to slack.

I can never ease off, not even for a moment.

And especially not with a legend in our midst.

I steal another glance at Monsieur Dupont, and flush hot when I find him still watching me. His dark eyes are narrowed, his jaw tensed, and he stares at me with such intensity that my knees tremble.

I rescue my posture at the last moment, strengthening my

limbs. I cannot mess this up. Not more than I already have.

By the time we leave the barre and step into the center, I feel one thousand years older. Every fumbled step, every wobble of my ankle, and misery churns worse in my gut. The worst part is Monsieur Dupont's heavy gaze, settled like iron weights on my shoulders.

I idolize this man.

The clips of his performances have stolen my breath; have brought moisture brimming in my eyes.

And now he's playing witness to what is quickly becoming the worst moment in my career. Why won't he show mercy and look away?

"Enough."

We freeze as the first bars of music stutter to a halt. Spaced in three lines in the center of the studio, we hold our breath as one. Even Madame, with her hardened eyes and pursed lips, seems to falter at Monsieur Dupont's tone.

"A moment, please." The way he says it, it's not a request. It's a command wrapped up in manners.

"Of course, Monsieur." Madame's hand flutters at the base of her throat. She marches to the piano, her palm slapping down on the wood. "Listen, class. Give Monsieur Dupont every scrap of your attention."

As if we would not. What a nonsensical command. Monsieur Dupont's eyebrow twitches, like he too finds the notion insulting, but he spares her further embarrassment.

No. All the humiliation is saved for me.

"Girl." His eyes fasten on me. "With the ladder in her tights."

Shame floods hot over my cheeks. I nod slightly to show I'm listening.

"Come here." He points to the front row. "In the center."

I dart a nervous glance at Madame, flinching at her scowl. The front row is reserved for her favorites. For the dancers she's ear-marked for greatness. But even she does not dare to contradict Raphael Dupont, so I inch forward, my heart pounding against my breastbone.

Monsieur Dupont strides forward to meet me. He takes me by the arm, placing me in the center of the row. His grip is warm and firm, his face unreadable as I gaze up at him, lips parted.

A hiss echoes through the studio as he lowers his head. Murmurs in my ear, just for me.

"Your nerves are terrible, pretty dancer. Torn to pieces, just like your tights."

The reminder of my threadbare clothes makes my cheeks burn. I duck my head, so ashamed, but the warm pad of his thumb draws light circles on my forearm.

"Ah, no. No tears, sweet girl. Only deep breaths and beautiful dancing. Yes?"

I draw in a shuddering inhale and nod. He smiles, faint and brief, then steps back. Glares around the class like their stares offend him.

"Well?" He claps twice, hard. "Get to work."

Raphael

There is an angel in this class. Her soft hair glints golden in the sunshine spilling through the windows; her rosebud lips part on a sigh as she dances the arabesque, her movements like the slow spread of honey. I frown at her, transfixed, as the students progress through their exercises, trying and failing to pinpoint why she captivates me so.

She's not the most technically perfect.

She does not have the highest extension or the most arched feet.

She does not even have the best focus, her attention slipping regularly from the dance and landing on me. Usually, I would snarl in frustration at such lack of focus.

But I find I like this—her distracted gaze on me. The pink flush on her cheekbones when I catch her looking; the way her nipples bead against her thin leotard. I begin to will her to look, to miss a step again and glance at me with those big, wistful eyes.

What do you want from me, angel?

Whatever it is, I do not think I would mind giving it.

"Paige!" The old woman scolds my pretty dancer for the dozenth time, exasperation crackling through her voice. I can't blame her, not with how distracted the girl is, and yet my spine stiffens.

Perhaps it is my imagination, but I suspect Madame is harder on Paige than the others. She picks out more flaws and speaks more curtly. And Paige cringes in response, conditioned and ready like she is used to harsh words in this studio.

Harsh words are part of a ballet dancer's training.

Even so—I do not like that.

With her new position in the front row, it is more clear than ever that Paige is far beyond her peers. Though her technique needs improvement in some areas, she dances with so much feeling that I forget to breathe.

Her every movement aches with emotion. She is lightness; ethereal grace.

"Paige! You are a two ton elephant!"

I do not hide my fury when I turn to Madame. She cringes back against the piano, her fingers scrabbling over the wood.

"Perhaps we have different ideas of greatness." I snap. Madame swallows hard, her powdered throat bobbing.

"No, Monsieur. Of course not! But the girl—she is losing time, she lands like a sack of bricks—"

"We are watching the same class," I tell her coolly. "Though I confess, I am not sure what *you* bring to the room."

I am being unforgivably rude. Several dancers stumble, picking up the moves again with wide eyes. And though Madame gapes at me, her mouth opening and closing like a fish, she has no retort.

I turn back to the class, chest tight. And find Paige staring at me, horrified, her face chalky white.

"Paige." I mouth her name—my lips move but no sound comes out. And something steely passes over her expression, her eyes hardening as her shoulders tense.

Her message is clear as she finishes the class with a tight jaw, refusing to meet my eyes.

My outburst was not welcome.

And now my angel won't look my way.

* * *

The second class I attend is no better. I should not even be here—one class was favor enough. But when I returned to my hotel suite last night, I could barely stand still with so much primal energy crackling under my skin.

The way she danced…

Those big, wistful eyes…

Perfection.

I am haunted by the little dancer from the class. And I will not leave until I see her again—I *cannot*. I tell myself that I won't bother her, that I won't stare so much as this morning.

Just as long as I can see her again. Just one more time.

Last night, I prowled the length of my suite so many times, I almost wore a track in the floorboards. And when I finally gave in to the vicious urges brimming in my chest, leaning one shoulder against the wall and choking my cock until I burst in my hand—

It was her face I saw.

Her name on my lips.

Paige.

"Monsieur Dupont!" To her credit, Madame does not turn me away at the door, despite my rudeness yesterday. She smoothes a nervous hand over her hair, steel gray and scraped back into the traditional bun. "We did not expect you again so soon."

"I wish to direct the showcase."

The words are a shock, even to me. Since when do I care about some little academy performance? I am not a recruiter nor a director; it means nothing to me how well these students audition for the ballet world.

"Monsieur..." Madame trails off, lost for words. She swallows hard, her papery throat bobbing. But then she rallies herself again, pushing her shoulders back and down, and gives me a glowing smile. "How marvelous."

I've stolen her throne in this studio, but the canny woman knows what this means: her academy will receive far more interest with Raphael Dupont leading the showcase. More interest means more contracts for her dancers, more attention from wealthy parents. More money; more prestige.

I haven't even demanded a fee. Lovestruck fool.

The dancers murmur quietly amongst themselves in the far corners of the studio, oblivious to our conversation. Only one has even noticed me here again, and she frowns at me with her big doe eyes. She's sitting on the cold floor, tying the ribbons of one pointe shoe.

Her tights are flawless pink, clearly fresh out of the packet. Something clenches in my chest.

It doesn't matter, I want to tell her. *It doesn't matter if your clothes are worn or your hair escapes its bun.*

She is still a revelation. My blood pumps hotter at the mere sight of her.

"Which ballet?" Madame asks, her voice raised in a way which makes me think she has asked several times already. "Monsieur?"

I tear my eyes away from Paige.

"Swan Lake." I hold Madame's gaze. "The dance of the seductress."

Paige

Why is he here?

Raphael Dupont could be in any room of the art world. He could watch the star dancers of the biggest companies rehearse in their studios, casting a judgmental eye over their technique. He could attend galas and red carpets; he could judge competitions and give interviews.

So what is he doing *here?*

This academy is great. One of the best in the country, despite its small size. But it's still a class of students, far below Monsieur Dupont's pay grade.

His dark eyes land on me again.

I shiver.

He seems different today. More agitated, like he didn't sleep well. He can join the club—I went home last night, ranted to my roommates, then locked myself into my bedroom and tossed and turned until dawn.

I even tried to soothe myself. To run my palms over my heated skin; to touch myself in those forbidden places.

It didn't help. The sensations built, fast and hard, but they left me hollow afterwards. Still wanting.

Seeing Monsieur Dupont again this morning... those thrumming, tickly feelings below my navel come flooding back.

I roll my head, wincing at my stiff neck, and smile politely as the girl next to me chats about a movie she watched last night. I'm trying to listen, honestly, but my eyes keep dragging back to Monsieur Dupont like they are pulled on two invisible reins.

He smirks at me, secret and slow.

"Oh god," I murmur to myself, shifting on the floor to press my thighs together.

"Huh?" The girl next to me screws up her face. "What is it?"

I don't even have to lie. "Monsieur Dupont. He's back."

The girl's head whips around, and my teeth clench at her breathless sigh.

"He's so *handsome*, isn't he?"

I say nothing.

"He looks like he could pick you up and slam you against a wall."

I do *not* need that mental image, nor the answering pulse between my legs. I huff and shove my last pointe shoe on, tying the ribbons with vicious tugs.

"You will cut off circulation."

I hear his deep voice before I notice the sudden hush around me. Monsieur Dupont crouches beside me, taking my foot in his big hands. He reties my ribbons with deft, sure motions, the pad of his thumb sweeping to circle quickly over my ankle bone.

I gape up at him, lips parted. His mouth quirks up on one side.

70

"Do not strangle your feet, Paige." He remembers my name? "They are a dancer's best friend."

His hands are still on my foot. Their heat scorches through my thin tights, burning into my skin. I blink up at him, drowning in the sensations of his touch, until my neighbor elbows me in the ribs.

"Oh! Um. Thank you, Monsieur Dupont."

"You are welcome." He lets go of me with clear regret, pushing to stand. *Oh my god,* the other dancer mouths at me, but I shrug.

I have no idea what is going on.

All I know is, this man caused me trouble yesterday. He singled me out with that heated gaze, made me clumsy and off-time and *aching* for something, then he embarrassed Madame on my behalf.

One day soon, he will leave, and I will be left with the consequences. So I drop my chin and stare resolutely at the floor.

It doesn't matter if this legend has taken an interest in me. He will leave soon, like everyone does, and I will be left in the wreckage.

He's brought me nothing but pain.

* * *

"The black swan's dance is wicked and wild. She is a seductress, sent to ruin the prince and make him forget all about his love."

I pick at my thumbnail as Monsieur Dupont explains the piece for the showcase. Some prince, if he forgets his love so easily.

"It is a pas de deux, a dance between partners, but more than that—it is a slide into temptation and chaos."

Sounds familiar. I fold my arms over my chest, staring at a spot on the wall over Monsieur Dupont's shoulder. It's safer this way, if I don't look him in the eyes. If I only listen to his deep voice with half my attention.

If I take in the full effect of him, I'm liable to crumble like that stupid prince.

And how humiliating would that be? A student dancer swooning over the ballet master. He wouldn't give me a second thought.

We pair off quickly at his command, seeking out our usual assigned partners. Madame mixes things up sometimes, but we mostly stick to our pairs. We've been matched for body size, style and temperament.

Monsieur Dupont's gaze burns the back of my neck as I cross the studio to my partner David.

"Cool showcase piece." David holds out his fist and I bump it.

"Yeah. Definitely."

David drops into a stretch, his muscles bulging and his joints popping. His light brown hair flops forward, so ashy compared to Monsieur Dupont's dark hair, and I look away quickly before I can draw more comparisons.

"Dupont seems to like you," David says suddenly.

I hum, noncommittal. It is not always a blessing to receive extra attention.

"Be careful there."

I look at David sharply, but his face is open. Innocent. Only creased in concern—for me. And why shouldn't he worry, when I can still feel Monsieur Dupont's glare burning into my skin even as we speak?

"I will." I lower my voice to a whisper. "I must remind him of someone."

David snorts, like I've said something funny. And he blushes as he says, "I doubt it."

How strange. I begin to ask him what he means, but Monsieur Dupont claps twice and we all jump to attention.

The showcase is *it*. My only chance for a great career.

I cannot afford any distractions.

Raphael

God, I am a fool. I've arranged my own torture: watching Paige in the arms of another man. She dances the steps perfectly, her movements lithe and primal, a secret extra swivel to her hips and smile curling her lips.

She's the perfect black swan. Half the men in this room are panting just watching her, and I tuck my fists behind my back to hide the whitened knuckles.

The way she dances… it's more erotic than a strip tease. More tantalizing than any burlesque. She dips into a back bend, and a groan rumbles through my chest.

Paige. Fuck. I'd give anything to touch her.

"What do you think, Monsieur?" Madame drifts up to my elbow. "Have you found your star pair?" Her eyebrow twitches, like it's a nonsense question. Like it's already clear who I'll choose.

I don't care.

"Yes. Paige and… that boy."

"David," Madame supplies.

Whatever. It's not like anyone will be watching *him.* The only thing he brings to the dance is his supporting arms, lifting Paige, and the shocking contrast of his big hands on her tiny waist.

My grip on her would be bigger still. I could perch her on my shoulder like a canary. I scrub a hand over my face, like I might erase such an image. As if I could stop myself picturing it—the slight weight of her, the warmth of her skin, the scent of her arousal, so close to my nose. Spinning her around until her legs spread around my head, and I could bury my face in that damp strip of leotard—

"David has wonderful technique," Madame puts in. "Truly, he is the stronger of the pair."

"If you value technique above soul," I mutter.

As if to demonstrate my point, David picks up Paige with such robotic motion, with so little feeling, that I stifle a snarl. Before I know what I'm doing, I stride across the studio, barking for the dancers to get out of my way.

"Stop." David's eyes widen as I reach them, and the pair stumble to a halt. Paige is breathing hard, her small tits heaving beneath her leotard, and I drag my eyes back to David with effort. "You are lifting a beautiful woman. Making love to her through dance. Why do you seem half asleep?"

David splutters, cheeks flaming, but I nudge him out of the way.

"I will show you."

The pianist begins again, fumbling the keys in his haste, but we pick up the rhythm quickly. Dancing with Paige is as easy as breathing—as easy as speaking to one another. *Easier* than that, in fact. Because when we speak through words, there is room for misunderstanding. For saying the wrong thing or taking offense.

When we dance together, our bodies cannot lie. There is no hiding the truth of our searing attraction for each other, our bodies twining and spinning and grasping like this is our one chance to express how we feel.

I break away from the choreography without thinking, grasping Paige by the ass and lifting her to wrap her legs around my waist. These are not the steps, this is not even ballet, but I could not put her down or unwrap her legs if I were held at gunpoint. We keep dancing, following our own secret steps, wrapped so tightly around each other that we almost blur into one.

A throat clears. Paige jerks in my arms, her eyes widening as though she is waking from a dream. She pushes at my chest, suddenly frantic, and I set her down, gut clenching.

Taking my hands off her warm, lithe body is the hardest thing I have ever done.

"You see," I rasp, turning to David. "Put some feeling into it."

He nods, as dazed as the rest of the class. Even Madame leans against the piano, a gnarled hand fanning her cheeks.

Paige scowls at me. "Is that the new choreography?"

I tilt my head. "Do you prefer it?"

Heat crawls up her neck, and I fight the urge to bend down and lick its path. But her voice is steady. "No. I don't like your version."

She's lying, the words ringing false through the studio, but I know why she says it—to protect herself from rumor. From my careless actions.

"Quite right." I force a smile. "Continue with the original steps."

Whispers break out as I walk back to the center of the class, and only my thunderous expression when I turn makes them scurry back to work.

I should not have done that. Should not have danced with her like that in front of everyone—as though our thin layers of clothing were the only thing keeping our bodies from joining.

Paige can lie to *them* but not to me. I heard the hitch in her breath; I saw her pulse tapping frantically against her throat.

I felt the damp heat between her legs.

She wants me too.

* * *

"You shouldn't have done that. You shouldn't have danced with me that way in front of everyone."

Her voice is quiet in the empty studio. It's risky for her to sneak back after class, and I scan the windows quickly before striding to shut the door. Paige stands in the center of the studio, her arms wrapped around her middle as her satchel hangs limp off her shoulder. A full day's dancing has made her skin flushed and dewy, and her poor muscles must ache.

I remember that. The pain of a day's training.

I miss it badly sometimes, but not right now.

Right now, I'm too busy devouring Paige with my eyes. Taking in every flushed, trembling inch of her.

"What about alone?"

"Huh?" She blinks, confused. Gives her head a little shake, like she got caught up daydreaming the same way I did. "What do you mean?"

"You said I shouldn't dance with you that way in front of

everyone. What about alone, angel?"

Her chest heaves under her baggy sweatshirt. All ballerinas do this—swamp their delicate frames in big, chunky layers.

As if Paige could hide the perfect slope of her hip. Her delicate limbs and strong muscles.

"I... I..." Paige wets her bottom lip, glancing at the door. Then, so quietly I almost miss it: "I guess that would be okay."

I'm already striding to meet her. Tugging her bag strap off her shoulder and setting her things carefully on the floor.

"But there's no music..."

"We don't need music."

"Someone might see—"

"Let them," I growl. She's offered me this, and now I can't bear it if she takes it back. But my Paige doesn't torment me. She lifts her arms, welcoming my embrace.

We dance the steps from earlier. But slower. More teasing. Paige's sneakers squeak on the floor, her sweater bunching at her shoulders, but it is perfection. Perfection.

I don't change anything this time—I've pushed her enough—so my heart almost stops when she breaks away from the steps. Paige dances closer, rougher, her hips cleaving to mine. She gazes up at me, her pupils blown and lips parted.

"What do you want from me, angel?" I rasp, following her lead into this new, dangerous territory. I grip her tightly, freely, my hands roaming over her tiny body. She is so small, a strong breeze could whip her away. "Do you need something?"

She whimpers. *"Yes,* Monsieur."

"Call me Raphael."

"Raphael. *Please.*"

I keep dancing even as my heart slams against my ribcage, loud enough to set our beat. I dip her back, her long legs stretched and pointed, and hover my lips an inch above her quivering breast bone.

"Tell me, angel. You have to say the words."

She huffs, frustrated as I swoop her back upright. "I don't *know* the words."

I grin, savage, as I scoop her up and crush her to my chest. Her legs wrap around my waist, our hips slotting together.

It's just like earlier, but now we're alone. There's no one to stop us. It's a heady feeling, and if I didn't have the weight of her in my hands, I'd think I was dreaming. The studio is silent, filled only with our breaths and the distant rumble of traffic that drifts through the walls.

"I thought you didn't like this version." I can't resist prodding her.

She rolls her eyes, and that show of spirit thrills me to my bones.

"You are cocky, Monsieur."

"Not with you." My smile dims. "You have knocked me off kilter, angel. But here are the words you need: *I want you to touch me, Raphael.*"

She wets her lip and repeats in a whisper. "I want you to t-touch me, Raphael."

"*I want your hands on my pussy.*"

"I want your h-hands on my pussy."

"*I want you to lick me until I scream.*"

"I want you to—" She breaks off, cheeks flaming. Clears her delicate throat. "I want that too."

Triumph flares inside me, so bright that beams of light should burst from my eyes. But I am only a man, so there are no godly beams of light—only my satisfied grunt and my quick steps to the studio wall. I rest Paige's ass on the wooden barre, smirking as her gaze snags on the mirrors behind us.

"That's right, angel. Watch me make you squirm."

She's swaddled herself in a thousand layers, the little tease, and for a split second I consider tearing them down the middle. But she'd have to leave the studio exposed and vulnerable, and I dismiss the thought quickly.

I will unwrap her like the gift she is.

"Wait." She tugs my shirt at the shoulder once I've peeled her leggings down and draped them over the barre. "You forgot something, Monsieur. You haven't kissed me yet."

My heart twists inside my chest, painful and wrenching, and I almost stagger to the side.

"Of course. Forgive me, angel."

I did not forget. It was the first fantasy that crossed my mind yesterday when I saw her in the studio. Tipping her pointed chin back and bringing my mouth down on hers; sliding my tongue between those pink lips.

But I never dreamed that she would want *this* from me. Comfort as well as physical relief. And my heart is in danger of shattering to pieces as I step between her spread thighs and cradle her face in my hands.

"I have more words for you to repeat."

Another eye roll, but a smile too.

"Oh?"

"Yes. Repeat after me: *I have ruined the ballet master. I have broken his old, tired heart.*"

She opens her mouth, then closes it again.

"I don't think I can say that," she whispers.

"No?" I duck my head, pressing a kiss below her ear. "Then I will say it for you." My lips blaze a trail up her flushed throat. Along her fine jaw until they meet her plump lips. Paige sucks in a sharp breath, moaning into my kiss and scrabbling at my shoulders.

I can't help myself—I nip her bottom lip between my teeth. I slide my tongue into her wet heat. But Paige welcomes me, kissing me back just as hard, her small body swaying in my grip.

"These layers," I growl, reaching down to find her leotard and tights still between us. I tug her sweatshirt over her raised arms, stripping her quickly. "They will drive me insane."

Paige lifts her hips as I pull her leotard and tights down her body, settling her ass back on the barre with only a pink thong left. The scrap of fabric taunts me, a damp patch spreading between her thighs.

I look up and find goosebumps rippling over her bare skin. With a rueful glance at her pert nipples, I settle the chunky sweatshirt back over her arms.

"It's cold," I grunt when she smiles at me softly.

"Warm me up then, Monsieur."

Paige

⁓◦⟨◦⟩◦⁓

Who is this man, treasuring me and wrecking me in equal measure? It's not the legendary dancer I watched on so many video clips, nor the gruff master who taught class today. He smiles at me, eyes crinkling at the corners, even as he runs his palms over me with the kind of ownership that steals the breath from my lungs.

He is commanding. Sure of himself. And his touch—it breaks me apart.

First, he slides his hands inside my baggy sweatshirt. His palms are warm and dry, dwarfing my rib cage, and I shiver as his fingertips graze the underside of my breasts.

"These tell me everything, don't they angel?" He rubs the pad of his thumbs over the hard beads of my nipples. I whimper, my forehead dropping into his shoulder, and he growls in approval. "Every time you look over at me in class, these gorgeous little tits strain against your leotard."

I should be embarrassed about that, but I can't think straight right now. Not with Monsieur Dupont's commanding touch on my skin, and his hips moving to slot against mine.

There it is again: the hard length in his dark pants. The thing I felt pressing against me secretly in class.

I bite my lip, face still buried in his shoulder, and roll my hips against him. Just to see how it feels.

Monsieur Dupont hisses between his teeth. "Careful, angel. This is about you. Don't try to distract me, now."

He steps away again, and my back stiffens. I want him flush against me, like he promised with his dance. I want the pulsing feeling below my navel to get stronger again. But I barely have time to lift my head and scowl before he's kissing me again, groaning against my lips.

"Don't frown at me, Paige." A broad fingertip traces the seam of my thong. I whimper and shift on the barre. "Not when I'm touching your pretty pussy."

He's not touching it yet, and now who's the tease? But before I can point that out, he slips his fingertip under the fabric.

The barest touch. That's what he gives me. And I guess it makes sense—the man is a ballet legend, and this dance is all about restraint. Iron-clad control. He teases me, the whisper of his touch along my slit enough to make heat explode over my skin.

I'd like to make him lose control. I'd like to make him messy.

The thought slips away as quickly as it came. Because Monsieur Dupont—Raphael—he finds the most sensitive spot. The tight bud of nerves at the top of my slit. And he rubs me there, firm and demanding, barking out a laugh when I groan and bite down on his shoulder.

"Rough little dancer. Look at you, scratching and biting the ballet master." I bite down harder, my teeth digging into his shoulder muscle, and he chuckles as he slides one knuckle deep into my pussy. "I knew you were a fighter, Paige. Not so shy at all."

My hips jerk, forcing him deeper, and he works his finger, rubbing at my walls. Two knuckles become three; one finger becomes two, until he's plunging both deep inside me. I lean my temple on his shoulder, watching our reflection in the mirror. The shameless rock of my hips, and the bulging tendon in his neck.

"Do you feel good, angel?"

I moan and nod, my vision blurring. I'm far past words.

"Then it's time."

He kneels so quickly, I'd topple off the barre if it weren't for his grip on my thigh. And he doesn't even bother to pull my thong down—just yanks it to the side and buries his face between my thighs.

His groan vibrates through my pussy. His tongue is searching, delving, rough. He laps at me like I am the most delicious treat—like I am dripping with the finest of champagnes. His eyes track up my body slowly until they fix onto mine, and my mouth rounds in a silent 'O' as he plunges his tongue deep inside me.

"M-Monsieur—"

"*Raphael*," he growls against my core.

"Raphael. I… I'm going to…"

I don't have time to finish my warning. Pleasure flashes hot through my body, searing and bright, and I twist my hands in his dark hair.

My wail echoes through the empty studio, bouncing off the mirrors. All around me, reflections of myself tip their heads back, mouth parted at the ceiling, and Monsieur Dupont's broad back flexes between the reflections' legs, his muscles shifting as he pushes me harder, deeper, *more.*

His fingers grip my thigh hard enough to bruise.

Distantly, I hope they do.

And when Monsieur Dupont stands again, long after my twitching subsides, he's breathing even harder than me. He lifts me down gently, settling me on wobbly legs, and fixes my sweatshirt so that it lays straight.

Only then does he wipe his chin, his mouth slick from my pussy.

"Perfect," he grits out, his voice like gravel. "I knew you would be. Like something from a dream."

A pleased blush adds to the inferno on my cheeks, but when I reach for the length still pushing against his pants, he bats me gently away.

"No, angel. This was about you." He steps back, scrubbing a hand over his face, and his rabid hunger fades. His face becomes cooler again, pleasant and controlled—he is the ballet master once more. No more Raphael.

Monsieur Dupont hands me the pile of my clothes.

"Now get dressed before you catch a chill."

* * *

"Before you *catch a chill?* Seriously, how old is this guy?" My roommate Leona wrinkles her nose at me from her seat on the kitchen counter. An open pizza box rests in her lap, the hot slices lying forgotten.

"Your pizza is going cold."

She rolls her eyes but picks up a slice. The molten cheese

stretches, pulling away in strings, and my stomach growls loudly.

"Want some?"

"No, thank you."

I cannot afford a cheesy pizza. Not even a single slice. For ballet, I must be strict about what I let inside my body.

An image flits across my brain: Raphael Dupont's tongue sliding between my folds. My breath catches.

Leona whistles. "What the hell did you just think of?"

"Nothing. Shut up." She cackles as I tug the refrigerator open, unoffended by my harsh words. Leona and I have lived here with our friend Avery for nearly two years. They know me better than anyone.

I frown at the tubs of chopped salad I prepared yesterday.

That pizza smells so good. Like hot dough and melted cheese and oregano.

"Come on." Something pushes into my hand—the pizza box. "One piece won't hurt. Then you can have your rabbit food."

I hesitate before choosing a small piece. Nibbling a tiny bite. Flavor bursts over my tongue, savory and delicious, and I stifle a groan.

It's my second forbidden pleasure of the day.

"Thank you."

Leona grunts, tearing off a bite of her crust. Her dark wavy hair hangs over her shoulders in two loose bunches, and her sketchpad rests on the counter by her hip. Leona understands my obsession with ballet, because she's the same way with drawing—she needs it like she needs air to breathe.

"He's in his thirties," I tell her, answering her question from earlier. "So, older than us. But not *old* old."

"Old enough to be sexy." Leona waggles her eyebrows. "Old

enough to know what he's doing."

I think of his proprietary grip on me. The way he arranged me on the barre, so sure of himself, and brought me to such shimmering pleasure that I thought the mirrors might shatter.

"Yes." God, I sound strangled. "Old enough for that. But…" I trail off, embarrassed. How am I supposed to admit this? That I must have done something wrong; that he didn't want me enough to take his pleasure in turn?

"But?" Leona prompts.

I open my mouth but the words don't come. There's only creeping shame, spreading through my gut, settling heavy in my stomach.

What did I do wrong?

Did I disgust him somehow?

Could he read my inexperience in the way I touched him?

Even if he did—my shoulders stiffen—that should not have made a difference. I can't exactly help my inexperience, and everyone must learn at some point. Right?

"Nothing," I grumble, pausing to gnaw at my pizza again. "It doesn't matter."

Leona watches me carefully, concern spreading through her brown eyes. She may seem pricklier than Avery and I, but Leona cares so much, I think she almost can't stand it.

"If he doesn't want you, he's an idiot." Her words are soft. Reassuring. But they still sting somewhere deep in my chest.

I shrug, forcing a rueful smile.

"It doesn't matter. He's the ballet master. I'm a student dancer. It couldn't work anyway."

Raphael

❧

There is something wrong with Paige.

The first day in the theater usually bubbles with excitement. The dancers can imagine it properly for the first time: the rows of faces in the audience. The music floating up from the orchestra pit. The heat of the lights and the deafening applause.

The rest of the dancers chatter excitedly as Madame and I lead them through the backstage corridors, giggling and whispering as we pass the stars' dressing rooms. And none have more reason to be excited than Paige—she has the biggest part. The most to gain.

Yet she trails behind the others, barely listening to whatever her partner David is droning about in her ear. Her eyes skate along the scuffed linoleum floor, the flyers pinned to cork boards fluttering as she walks past.

Her shoulders are slumped. Her face is pale.

My God, what have I done?

"The costume fittings are scheduled for 3pm." Madame lists

the day's appointments in my ear, but I cannot concentrate either. Not when my angel is dragging her feet over the corridor floor, so lost and deflated.

Did I hurt her?

Did I—did I *force* her somehow? Make her feel obliged to me—the ballet master? Bile rises in my throat at the thought. It felt so perfect in the studio yesterday, the two of us falling into flawless sync when we were alone—did I imagine that?

God.

If I have harmed my angel… I cannot live with myself.

"I must speak to the leads."

I contain myself until we are gathered on the stage, the dancers gaping at the scenery hanging in the flies overhead. But as soon as Paige's eyes land on me, I can't wait a moment longer. I need to speak with her. I need to *know*.

"The rest of you warm up. Run through the steps. We will block out the opening dance."

I barely hear my own instructions. I can only see Paige, can only watch the gentle rise and fall of her chest beneath her sweater. Her chunky sweatshirt is gone today—she is draped in a soft black woolen sweater which brushes against the dips and swells of her body.

Perfect for the black swan.

She is perfect.

"Paige. David." I clear my throat. "Come here, please."

David strides quickly over, but Paige drags her feet. She walks to me like she is walking to the gallows, and pain ripples through my chest.

"Are you ready?" I croak. She won't *look* at me.

"Yeah, definitely," David says brightly. "I'm so psyched."

Fine. Whatever. I am happy that David is *psyched*, but can

he not see that his partner is wilting?

"Give us a moment please, David." Enough pretense. His eyes widen, but he walks away without another word. He joins the nearest group of dancers, dropping his bag to the floor and beginning his stretches, glancing back over his shoulder.

"Yes, Monsieur Dupont?"

Her voice is so quiet.

"Raphael," I grit out. "Why do you not use my name?"

She looks up then at last, anger sparking in her eyes.

"Because we are in rehearsals, Monsieur. And here, I have no right—"

"You have *all* the right." I step closer, hands itching to reach for her. "You more than anyone."

She blinks, surprised, but then sets her chin again.

"This is my career, Monsieur. I want to be professional."

She's right. She's quite right, and I know that she is, but I still hate this distance between us. If we were alone again, like we were in the studio, I could crush her to my chest. I could trail my lips along her hairline, I could suck in great lungfuls of her fresh cotton scent—

"What happened yesterday…" I need to know. "Did I force you, angel? Did I make you unhappy?"

"Um." She darts a nervous glance around. Turns back to me, confused. "No. Of course not. At least…"

I clench my hands into fists. "At least what?"

She bites her lip. Answers in the smallest whisper. "At least until you pushed me away."

"Pushed you—"

I dig my fists into my eyes. It is unthinkable.

"Paige," I manage. My chest heaves under my shirt. "Do you think I don't want you?"

"Um."

Jesus Christ. This is a disaster. But Madame claps her hands, apparently tired of my neglect of her class. She gathers the dancers into their places for the starting dance, marking spots on the stage with strips of tape.

Paige glances over her shoulder, her arms wrapped tight around her middle.

"I should get back to rehearsal, Monsieur."

"Of course." I cannot speak anyway.

She looks at me one last time, chewing on indecision. Then she murmurs: "Thank you for this opportunity, Raphael."

My heart flops over in my chest. The poor organ is too battered to do much more.

* * *

My chance comes hours later, when the afternoon sunshine filters through the open stage dock door and the dancers wilt with exhaustion. Madame is a taskmaster, barely allowing them enough breaks to sip their water bottles, but we have made excellent progress.

No one ever said ballet was easy.

I check my wristwatch, noting vaguely that my flight back to Paris will be landing around now, my seat in first class notably empty.

I don't care. Paige is *here*.

The academy's theater is small but refined. The seats can only hold a few hundred people, but every part of the building is well made. The cushioned seats are luxurious; the bars overhead bristle with stage lights; the wood panelled walls are glossy and fine.

"You will be called for your fittings in pairs," I tell the students. "Do not keep the dressers waiting." I school my features carefully blank. "Paige and David. You will be fitted first."

It's nothing unusual. And no one but Paige even blinks an eye when I fall into step beside them.

"You're attending the fittings?" David asks, but there's no layered meaning to his question. He is simply a friendly young man making conversation.

"Yes. For the leads." I don't care about the others. Madame will take care of them. I risk a glance at Paige, but she's staring at the floor again.

God help me. Her sadness twists a hook in my gut.

"I bet you wore some crazy costumes over the years."

I roll my eyes. "Yes, David." Costumes are most exciting for new dancers. When you start to win roles, when there are famous costumes you must wear, you find out that they are heavy and chafing. Often too delicate to clean properly, and stiff with other dancers' sweat.

This will not be a problem for Paige. I ensured it. I placed a call late last night.

My Paige is soft. Delicate. Beautifully scented. She will not dance in sweaty cast-offs.

"Fit him first," I tell the dressers when we step into Wardrobe. I nudge David forward, flashing a charming smile at the nearest seamstress. "Please."

"Of course." The woman flutters her hands for David to come closer, a long tape measure draped around her neck. "At once, Monsieur Dupont."

"Paige and I will be just outside." I take her by the elbow. "Running the steps one more time."

No suspicious eyes follow us. No harsh whispers echo through the room. The workers are too busy rifling through huge dress rails, speaking to each other through pins pinched between their lips.

"Is there a problem with the steps?" Paige asks as I tug her through the doorway.

"Not with the steps." I glance both ways along the corridor, then flatten her against the wall. She gasps, staring up at me with wide eyes. "My angel thinks I don't want her. I must show her how wrong she is."

Paige

"I don't understand."

He is *everywhere.* His broad shoulders block out the light as he crowds me against the wall. His chest hovers half an inch away, but his heat licks through my thin leotard.

"You—you didn't want me to touch you—"

"I'd *die* for you to touch me." The words burst out of him in a snarl, but I'm not afraid. Caged in here, my shoulder blades flush against the cool wall, with his warmth and the faint thump of his heartbeat…

My pulse calms.

"Really?"

Raphael's dark eyes narrow, boring into mine. For the first time, I let myself see the full force of his obsession. There's a glint to his eyes, a hard set to his jaw which says this is bigger than either of us.

It's primal.

Essential.

And suddenly I don't need his words. His reassurances.

Everything I wanted to hear is right there in his eyes. So I raise one eyebrow, lift a trembling hand, and cup the side of his face.

"Like this?"

His stubble scratches my palm. His strong cheekbone is firm under the sweep of my thumb, and his shudder vibrates right through me to the wall.

"Yes," he rasps. Steps a fraction closer. "Just like that, Paige."

"How about this?" I lift my other hand and rest it above his heart. His chest heaves, the muscles as firm as rock. I watch my own hand on him, dazed by the sight, by how small I look compared to him. Tiny and fragile.

I'm *not* fragile, though. And Raphael knows it. Because he growls and presses against me, urging our bodies flush and trapping my hand between us. Something juts against my hip—that hard length of him again—and I swallow a moan as I rock my hips towards him.

"We are in the corridor, Paige." He ducks his head. Nips my earlobe. "Where anyone could catch us. And here you are, moaning and writhing against me."

He's right. He's right. I can't get him close enough. I need his friction, his heat, I need *more.* I nod clumsily, tugging hard on his shirt.

"Yes. Please, Raphael."

He growls his approval, running the tip of his nose along my hairline. "There it is, angel. Say my name."

"R-Raphael."

His hips thrust hard against me. I try to slide a hand between us to touch him, but my limbs are pinned and my head is swimming.

"Beautiful girl." He sucks my throat. "Soulful girl." His teeth scrape over my collarbone. All I can do is stand there and let him feast on me, let him turn my legs to jelly and my breath to quick gasps. "You're going to be fitted with wet panties, aren't you?" He shakes his head, chuckling. "Bad angel."

A door scrapes open further down the corridor, and Raphael steps away, swift and calm. He adjusts his sleeve as a technician walks past, grunting hello.

I sprawl against the wall, cheeks flushed and core throbbing. He's set an ache in me, and if he doesn't soothe it soon, I'll go insane.

"We're ready for you, dear." The voice by my shoulder makes me jump. A dresser stands in the doorway, her smile bright. She clucks when she sees my flushed red cheeks. "You've been working her hard, Monsieur Dupont."

He nods, face serious. "Yes. Paige needs a firm hand."

Laughter bubbles up in my throat, but I choke it back. His eyes twinkle at me as I turn to step through the doorway.

"Come straight back to rehearsals when you're done, Paige. I'm not finished with you."

* * *

The stage is silent. Dust motes hang in the air, spinning lazily in the evening light. The stage dock doors are flung open, distant traffic rumbling on the roads, but in here the loudest noise is the echo of past applause.

I drop my bag with a thump. Raphael didn't tell me to stay after rehearsals. He didn't need to. I read the command in his scorching gaze, in the way he dragged his thumb over his lip as he watched me dance.

The black swan. The seductress.

It suits me more than I thought it would.

The soles of my sneakers drag over the stage floor as I dance through the steps, arms floating through the air. My feet are clumsy in the shoes, but I can't risk kicking them off and dancing in my tights. It's slippery, plus there might be dropped nails or other dangers, and I can't risk my feet.

Like Raphael said. They're a dancer's best friend.

My breath comes faster as the steps become more urgent, the black swan's seduction growing more intense. I spin faster, leap higher, arch my back and toss my head. Then land with a soft thump, more clumsy than in my ballet shoes.

My breath saws in and out of my lungs, and I beam at the empty seats.

Soft claps echo from the stage wing.

"Beautiful. Of course."

Raphael's gaze is hungry as he prowls onto the stage, still clapping. His plans for me are written all over his face, but there is something I want to do first. So when he reaches me, arms already outstretched, I stop him with a palm on his chest.

"Wait. Dance with me first."

He grinds out a laugh. "Paige. You are a torment." But he seems pleased as his posture changes, moving into a dancer's pose, and he sweeps me into his arms. Though he does not dance on stage anymore, Raphael is still breathtaking. A force of nature, so powerful and full of grace.

He leads me through steps I don't recognize at first—certainly not the steps of the prince.

"The dance of the sorcerer," he murmurs, his mouth against my temple. As though he heard my thoughts out loud. "The wicked magician who corrupts the younger woman."

I smile, my eyes fixed on his chest. "You're not wicked."

"No?" He grips me by the ass suddenly, lifting me and sealing our hips together. "How about now?"

His length nestles against the seam of my leggings, so big and hard and demanding. And if he is wicked then so am I, because I moan and rub against him.

"Do you feel that? Do you feel what you do to me?" His words are strained, spoken into my hair.

"Yes." I bite my lip. "I need it."

Raphael curses darkly, striding off stage and into the darkness of the wing. Huge black drapes hang from the ceiling, creating shadowed alleys and secret hideaways. Raphael carries me into an alcove, still urging me to rub against him, swallowing my moans with his kiss.

One hand leaves my ass. I wind my arms around his neck as he shifts his grip, holding me steadier. Then gentle fingers probe at the waistband of my leggings.

"Ah, Paige." He rests his forehead against mine, rocking his head from side to side. "These layers. You are testing me."

"You could tear them." I don't know where the words come from. They bubble up out of me, unbidden. And it makes no sense—I don't have so many clothes that I can throw them away like that—but Raphael shudders out a sigh and shakes his head.

"Not here. Another time." His mouth quirks up. "I will buy you such pretty replacements. And you can model them for me angel, practicing your dance—"

We're getting so far ahead of ourselves.

Another time?

Modeling for him?

He makes it sound like this will happen again. Like we could be a—a *couple*—something more than a dirty little secret. Hope swells in my chest, fierce and sudden, and I give him a bruising kiss.

Yes. I want that. I know it's risky, that it will complicate things...

But it's also simple between us. So, so simple.

"I will be patient," he sighs. "Even though my heart might give out." I pluck at his sleeve, alarmed, but he winks at me, teasing. Raphael puts me down carefully, crowding me deeper into the alcove until my back is against the wall.

Here, we are wrapped up in shadows. But over his shoulder, the stage is lit up with evening light.

"You must be quiet." He draws my leggings down, dropping to kneel in front of me. I lean one hand on his shoulder as I step out of them. "Can you do that, angel?"

"Of course," I say, affronted. I'm not *that* wild with lust.

Raphael chuckles. "We will see."

He undresses me quickly, positioning himself so that his broad back would hide me from any interlopers. Cool air washes over my bare skin, my nipples pebbling and growing darker, and he lets out a growl before ducking to suck on one. His tongue lathes hot over the sensitive bud, sending a pulse between my legs.

"Shit." I squeeze my eyes shut, heat flooding my core.

Raphael snorts against my skin. "Language."

Raphael

My angel is full of surprises. Just when I think I understand her, when I think I can predict how she will react—she turns my world upside down.

Shit.

The naughty word trips off her tongue. What else can I make polite little Paige say?

If we were in my hotel suite, I would drag this out. Would make it last for hours and hours, only stopping to rub Paige's shoulders and bring her glasses of ice water.

But we're not in my suite. We're exposed, out in the open, and though that adds a sharp edge to my hunger, it also hurries me along.

I don't want Paige to get caught here with me. Nor do I want her to catch a chill. So I scoop her into my arms, backing her against the wall, and wait with gritted teeth as she fumbles with the button of my pants.

"Sorry—I can't—"

"It's alright. Relax, sweetheart." She sighs softly, melting in my arms, and tries again, slower this time. My button pops open and her pale hand reaches inside.

I hiss as her fingers close around me.

"You must be quiet, Raphael." Her voice is thick with amusement. "Can you do that?"

She drags her fingers from my root to my tip. Her grip is gentle, featherlight, and somehow that is more maddening than if she squeezed. I buck into her hand, flattening her back against the brick. It's cold against her flushed bare skin, and she shivers, squirming closer.

Yes.

This is heaven. This is all I'll ever need.

I balance Paige against the wall as I roll on a condom. She cannot dance if she falls pregnant, and I will not risk everything she has worked so hard for, never mind that I want to feel her against my skin so badly my teeth ache.

No. There will be plenty of time to make beautiful, caramel-haired babies.

A whole lifetime of my Paige.

She is warm and wet when I notch the head of my cock to her entrance. Her muscles twitch and pulse, urging me inside.

"Are you sure?"

I cannot believe I am asking that question.

Except—yes, of course I am. I would rather die than make her unhappy.

"Yes." She nods rapidly, her eyes already glazed. "Please. Hurry."

It's such a tight squeeze that spots of white flash over my eyes. I clench my jaw and push in slowly, her slickness easing the way. Every time Paige tenses, her breath coming faster, I pause and let her adjust.

I will not rush her.

Not even with my heart galloping in my chest.

When we are finally sealed together, her naked body sprawled against the brick, my clothing still intact—I screw my eyes shut and will myself not to come apart.

"Move." She tugs at my shirt, her voice thick. "Please, I—I need you to move."

"Needy angel." I twitch my hips forward, eyes still screwed shut, and smirk at her strangled moan. "Begging for my cock against a wall backstage. Dancing for me like such a little tease."

Paige whimpers, latching onto my neck and sucking hard enough to bruise. She's trying to mark me, to claim me as her own, and that knowledge makes my lip curl in a snarl. My hips snap harder, faster, and she bounces in my arms, sliding up and down on my cock.

"I'm yours, pretty girl. No need to be jealous."

"You're mine," she whispers. "You're mine."

It's another surprise, this possessive streak, but a good one. I offer her the other side of my throat to mark too.

"Show everyone." I punch my hips forward, slamming deeper inside her. She groans, tugging at my hair. "Stake your claim."

Feeling her little tongue lathe at my skin—feeling her teeth scrape—I blow out a hard breath and steady one hand on the brick. She bounces on my cock, clinging to my shoulders and working herself up and down, and she's so hot and sweet that I see stars.

Crack.

My palm glances off her ass, reddening the skin. Paige whimpers, squirming in my arms to fuck me faster, harder, her eyes unfocused and bright.

"That's it," I say, ragged. "Climb me, wildcat."

The truth is, I can barely believe this is real. She feels too tight and wet; her moans are too sweet; her nails digging into me are the perfect bite of pain.

I used to find heaven in dance.

Now it's pumping its hot pussy on my cock.

"I'm going to keep you," I tell her raggedly. "Would you like that, angel?"

She hiccups and nods, working her hips faster, faster.

"Show me." I slide a hand between us and rub her clit. "*Show me.*"

Paige comes with a hoarse cry, her legs twitching around my hips. She bites my shoulder again, the little fiend, and the sharp points of those teeth drive me over the edge too.

"*Angel,*" I growl, thrusting inside her in three deep, slow strokes. I hold there, emptying into her heat.

My ears ring as sounds fade back in. First, there is our ragged breathing. Then the distant rumble of traffic out on the road.

Then heels drumming over the stage.

"Quickly." I pull out with a wince and put Paige down. I barely have time to snatch up her clothes and push her naked body behind a drape, to tuck myself away condom and all, before Madame calls out my name.

"Monsieur Dupont! There you are." She eyes the empty alcove closely as she walks near. "I've been looking for you."

I stride out to meet her, away from the smell of sex lingering in the air. Away from Paige, hidden and vulnerable.

"Madame. What is it you need?"

The woman leads me away, babbling about costumes and

lighting. I go with a frustrated glance over my shoulder, every atom in me screaming out to stay with Paige.

To dress her. Hold her. Kiss her forehead.

Damn this meddling woman.

"Make this quick," I mutter. "I have matters to attend to."

"In that alcove?" Madame asks lightly.

I stare at her, but her weathered face is blank. Innocent.

"In my hotel."

It's true. I plan to run a bubble bath for Paige. To feed her strawberries and champagne.

"Of course, Monsieur." Her heels drum faster across the stage. "I have my own business to attend."

Paige

❦

The alcove is icy cold once Raphael's warmth is gone. I dress quickly and silently, shivering in the dark, nerves gathering in my stomach.

What we did…

I'd been so happy. It felt so *right*. But alone now, quietly dressing like some shameful secret…

I bite my lip and pull on my clothes faster.

I wait for Raphael in a dressing room. It's empty now, the counters cleared and the room cloaked in shadows, but it will be mine soon. For the showcase.

My moment as the black swan.

I wrap my arms around my waist and squeeze. This is good. It's good. I've been cast as the lead, and Raphael held me like I was precious.

So why is there a pit of dread growing in my stomach?

When the door scrapes open, I blow out a relieved breath and smile, hopping down off the counter. But it's not Raphael who marches into the room.

"Madame," I splutter. "I was—I was just—"

She holds up a gnarled hand. "Do not lie to me." Her black-ringed eyes rake over me and she purses her lips. "Come on."

"Come where?" I follow her in a daze through the theater corridors, my bag bouncing against my hip. "Madame?" I can still feel Raphael between my legs. I grit my teeth and walk faster.

"I cannot teach bad girls. You will bring shame to the academy."

I stumble, my heart slamming against my rib cage.

"Madame," I gasp. "Please…"

"Did he tell you he loves you?" She sneers over her shoulder, not breaking stride. "Foolish girl. Powerful men will say anything to get between a pretty girl's thighs."

I swallow hard, my tongue thick. Because the truth is even worse—Raphael didn't even tell me that. He called me sweet names and said he would keep me. But love?

Have I thrown everything away for one embrace in the wings?

"Please, Madame." I ball my hands into fists to stop from grabbing the back of her sweater. "I've worked so hard. This doesn't affect my dancing—"

"Of course it does," she scoffs. "Do you think he would have cast you if he did not want to bed you?" She sniffs. "Though *bed* was a bit beyond you, clearly."

My breath saws in and out of my lungs.

I can't breathe. I can't breathe.

Madame leaves me on the stage docks, the wind tugging at my hair. I don't even deserve the front door. And that is where Raphael finds me, my lips numb and my face tingling, but not from the cold.

106

"Paige!" He jogs over, a smile stretching his cheeks. Oh god, he's so handsome. Even now, my sore heart flips over in my chest. "Ready to go, angel?" He grips my hips, kneading the bones as his voice drops. "I want to show you my suite."

More sex. More seduction.

Oh god, what have I done?

I bat his hands away, anger and despair climbing my throat. "Don't touch me!"

"Paige?" He reaches for me again, then remembers my command. His hands hover in midair, partway to my waist. "What's wrong?"

"What's wrong?" My cold laugh bounces around the dock. The wind whistles along the theater wall. "You've cost me *everything*, Raphael. Everything. I threw away my only chance to dance for one fumble backstage."

His forehead creases. His voice hardens. "What are you talking about?"

I wave a hand, impatient. I can't say it out loud. I *can't*. And he's a smart man—he can read between the lines.

We're caught. And I'm the one to pay the price.

My career, gone. My future, gone.

I've been so stupid.

"I will fix this." He cradles my face, sweeping away a tear with his thumb. "It is my fault. I will fix it, angel."

I gather the last scraps of my dignity. Build a wall around my poor, shattered heart. And shove him away by the chest, gritting my teeth at the hurt flashing across his face.

"I don't want *anything* from you." My voice is hollow, but it carries. And Raphael flinches, his face going pale. "I never want to see you again, Monsieur Dupont."

I leave him there like Madame left me.

And I make it half a mile before I burst into tears.

* * *

"Oh my god." Leona ushers me into the apartment, pulling my bag off my shoulder. "Avery!" she yells into the living room, then turns to me. "What happened?"

I sniffle, too ashamed to say the words. I can only shake my head, mute.

"Did he hurt you?" Avery clatters into the hallway behind Leona, her blonde hair scraped into a French braid. The two of them are puffed up, ready to pick a fight.

I think of the gentle way Raphael held me. The worshipful look in his eye as he slid inside me, sealing us together.

"No," I rasp. "But I'm out of the academy." I suck in a shuddering breath. "I've lost everything. I'll never be a dancer."

They hiss, faces twisting. They know how much this hurts me. How hard I've worked for ballet.

"We'll fight it," Leona says at once. "We'll campaign. Or kick up a fuss. There must be something we can do."

I shake my head, lip wobbling, and they both deflate. Avery takes my elbow and pulls me through to the living room.

"It'll be okay," she says softly. "There's more than ballet, Paige."

I scowl at my lap. She doesn't get it. Avery likes college, sure, but it's not her whole world. Especially since her hot professor changed jobs and became her boyfriend.

But Leona understands. Without her art, she'd go mad.

Just like I'm going now.

The worst part is, I'm not just sad about the ballet. It's been less than an hour, and I already miss Raphael so much that my heart throbs.

"We'll fight it," Leona says again. "We'll figure something else out. Another path to dance."

I nod, too numb to argue anymore, and Avery drapes a soft throw around my shoulders. They settle on either side of me on the sofa, both stunned into silence.

Leona clears her throat. "Well. You know what this means, right?"

"What?" I mumble. I'm suddenly so tired, I could sleep for years.

"Pizza." Her elbow jabs my ribs. "A whole one all to yourself."

It's silly, but a snort bursts from my mouth, and they both sag in relief at my sides.

"I'll get my laptop." Avery pops up, and Leona slings an arm around my shoulders. I rest my head back against the cushions.

"Leona?" I murmur at the ceiling.

"Yeah?"

I screw my eyes shut. "Don't forget the garlic bread."

* * *

Madame calls me at 10am the next morning. I answer the phone slowly, my voice thick from crying all night.

"Um. Hello?"

"You need to come back," she snaps without preamble. "He won't direct without you here."

She hangs up without another word and I stare at the phone in my hand, my heart thumping in my chest. My lips part ready to call for Leona, but it buzzes again in my palm.

"H-hello?"

"Paige Stevens? I'm calling from the East Coast Ballet Company. We'd like to arrange an audition."

The calls come all morning, one after the other. My week fills up with private auditions for incredible companies—the kinds of places I've always dreamed of working. My fingers shake as I write down the details, a weird buzzing sound in my skull.

After the fourth call, I put my pen down and pinch my arm. Ow.

Yeah, this is really happening.

I forget all about Madame's call until she rings again after lunchtime.

"What do you want?" she growls. "You already have the star role. Do you want new costumes? A private room to screw the director?"

It's my turn to hang up without a word. I toss my cell phone onto my bed with savage pleasure.

The one person I don't hear from is Raphael. I snatch up the phone each time it buzzes, eager to hear his voice, but it's always someone else. Another fantastic opportunity that he's clearly arranged for me, but not *him*.

I only want him.

I don't have his number. Don't know which hotel he's staying at. And I told him I never wanted to see him again.

"Oh god." I rub my eyes, too jangled up to think straight. "Raphael."

I need to find him. I need to make this right.

Raphael

The river sparkles in the evening light, snaking between the avenues below. I stand at the edge of the hotel roof terrace, a warm breeze tugging at my hair, and fill my lungs with a deep inhale.

Paige.

I gust out my breath.

It's done. I have solved the problems I caused her. There is nothing left to do now but return to the airport. My plane ticket is booked, my bags are packed, and yet I can't seem to force my feet to turn and go.

A life without Paige... Never seeing her dance again. Never making her sweet mouth sigh and utter bad words.

I can't bear it.

"Fuck." I tear my gaze away from the river and turn back to the terrace, ready to force myself to honor her wishes. She doesn't want to see me again, so I will not cause her trouble, even though my chest is one throbbing mass of pain.

A movement catches my eye. Graceful and slight.

It can't be.

Paige stands ten feet away on the terrace, watching me with unreadable eyes. Her pale blue dress whips in the breeze, floating around her legs, and goosebumps ripples over her crossed arms.

"Paige?" Her name is thick in my mouth. "Do you need something from me?"

Perhaps the name of a contact. Or a reference of some kind. Whatever she asks, I will give.

But Paige does not answer straight away. She cocks her head, watching me closely.

"These auditions..." She firms her shoulders. Clears her throat. "Are they real? You know... based on talent? You haven't bribed anyone, right?"

I straighten, affronted.

"Of course not." What kind of man does she think I am? "You will have to dance your best to be in with a chance."

She relaxes slightly, her eyes warming.

"Good," she whispers. "That's good." Her fingers pluck at her floaty skirt, but she doesn't say anymore. And though I hate to leave her presence, my flight is waiting.

"I must go." Her eyes widen, and though I shouldn't, I risk a step closer. If I could only catch her scent one more time, even *touch* her—but I will not be greedy. So I give her a polite smile. "My flight leaves shortly. If you need anything from me, you can reach me via my agent."

Her lip wobbles. I reach for her, gut churning, my hand hovering uselessly in the air. What the hell have I said now?

"You're going?" Her voice is so small. "When will you be back?"

Months. Perhaps years.

But there is something lost in her eyes. So I risk the question, even though her answer may hurt.

"When would you like me to come back?"

She scoffs, scowling at her feet. "Tomorrow," she says, so sullen. "As soon as you arrive, I want you to turn around and get back on the plane."

She is in a huff, my funny girl, so busy staring at the roof tiles that she misses my sudden grin.

She wants me to stay.

My heart—it might burst.

"Paige," I say carefully. "Come here, please."

She scuffs her sandal against the terrace. Her hands grip her elbows so tight, her fingertips turn white, and that's how I know that she is hurting.

Never again.

I've made enough mistakes for our lifetime.

"Paige." I put some command into the word, using the air of the ballet master. The man who calls the shots; who makes and breaks dreams. Her feet move automatically, before her brain realizes, and I snatch her close and hold her against my chest.

"I don't understand." Her words are muffled in my shirt. I kiss the top of her head, hard.

"I love you, angel. Do you understand that?"

She freezes. Then, all at once, her arms band tight around my waist.

"I love you too." The tip of her nose brushes my chest. "I'm so sorry, Raphael. I thought..."

"What?"

The tips of her ears turn red. "That it was about sex. Not love."

Even as she confesses her fears, her slight body pressed against my own makes my blood pump faster. Hotter. I duck my head, nipping at her earlobe.

"I see. Can it not be both?"

She sucks in a surprised breath, then melts against me, rubbing her hips against mine.

I chuckle. "I'll take that as a yes."

Paige

∽◌◌◌∽

Six years later

The applause is deafening. It beats against my ear drums and rattles my teeth. I drop into another curtsy, beaming so wide my cheeks ache.

I did it.

I danced the black swan.

My eyes slide backstage, to the man waiting in the wings. Raphael insists on attending every performance, though he quickly learned to watch from backstage so that the press don't mob him.

I like him back here, anyway. He's closer.

I can feel his eyes on me.

And between scenes, when I have breaks from being on stage, he sweeps me into hidden alcoves and kisses my neck. Feeds me sips of chilled water from my bottle and massages my legs.

He's watching me now, lust and adoration burning in his

dark eyes. Everyone can see it—the stage hands give him a wide berth, startled by his intensity.

My husband doesn't frighten me. He is simply a very passionate man.

"Hello, sorcerer." I wink at him when I finally run into the wings, my steps quick and delicate. "Have you come to corrupt your younger woman?"

"Always." He yanks me to his chest, never mind the sweat cooling on my skin, then licks a stripe up my throat. "Though I'm not sure any more who is corrupting who."

It's a fair point. Half the time, it's me seeking out Raphael and climbing his broad, toned body. I like to muss his hair. Make cracks in his iron-clad restraint.

I like to make the ballet master messy.

"You were perfect." He scrapes his teeth along my jaw. "Perfect. As always."

"I prefer dancing it with you," I murmur against his temple. A shudder ripples through Raphael.

"Let's go." He takes my hand and tugs me towards the dressing rooms.

"But I left my shoes—"

"Leave them."

"People are staring—"

"*Let them.*"

I grin, letting him tug me along. This is all part of it. Part of the game. I squeeze his hand and he squeezes mine back. The other dancers and stagehands duck out of our path, eyes wide, but I don't care.

He'll make me cry out anyway.

Raphael Dupont is legendary for a reason. He knows how to put on a show.

III

Life Model

Description

It's terrifying enough modeling for an art class in the city.

Then my professor walks in.

I've wanted my art professor since the day I met him. He's so calm, so assured, so stern. But he's only ever been distant. Polite and professional. That all changes the minute I drop my white robe.

We shouldn't be here. He shouldn't see me like this.

But I don't turn back.

And neither does he.

Leona

I drag my charcoal over the paper, relishing the soft scrape. The lump is warm between my fingers, staining my fingertips black so that I leave little smudges on the edge of the sketchpad.

It doesn't matter. I'll fix those later. With drawing, everything can be fixed.

As I work, everything gets better. My breathing slows. My tensed muscles relax. The endless worries buzzing around my mind—they go quiet. Soon, I'm not in a half-filled classroom in the art department, listening to the other students mutter to each other as they work. I'm not perched awkwardly on a wobbly stool, trying not to tip over as I sketch. I'm not *anywhere*.

I'm drawing.

"Good, Leona." A voice behind my shoulder jerks me back. Makes me twitch, my hand streaking charcoal over the paper. I grit my teeth, but I'm not annoyed at *him*.

I always make a fool of myself in front of the professor.

"I can't get the light." My hands tremble as I adjust my

sketchpad on its easel, leaving smudgy little fingerprints. I'll
fix the error when he's gone—when my heart slows and my
hands stop shaking.

When I can breathe again.

Professor Reeve hums, the sound deep and smooth, and I
bite down hard on my lip. The man has a voice that belongs
in cathedrals—vibrating stained glass and warming the stone
walls. The college art department is a small imitation of that,
housed in a renovated chapel, but it still makes him seem...
unearthly.

An ancient god.

It's ridiculous, of course. Professor Reeve is just a man, flesh
and bone like the rest of us.

"It's tricky with charcoals."

He's just saying that to be nice. But I don't point that out,
not when he leans over my shoulder, pointing at the table in
the center of the room. The still life is laid out in the style of a
renaissance painting—all waxy fruits, rippling tablecloth, and
water sparkling in a clear glass jug, with light cascading down
from the rafters in a bright shaft. I try to focus on where he's
pointing rather than his scent.

Soap. Spice. The earthy scent of clay.

Screw it. I suck in a deep, greedy breath of him, hooking my
ankles around the legs of my stool.

"The water is the focal point. Do you see? The light is
refracted and bounced around from there." Professor Reeve
keeps talking, showing me where to look, how to study the
scene before me with fresh eyes. And I listen, I do, but his deep,
smooth voice is half drowned out by my pounding heart.

Is it normal? Reacting to a man like this? Never any
others—just this one. I want to ask my friends if there's

something wrong with me, if I'm a tiny bit insane to be affected this much, but I'm too scared they'll tell me: *Oh dear. Yes. There's something wrong with you.*

"Lighten your hand here." Professor Reeve has turned back to my sketchpad. To my half-done drawing. I hold my breath as he looks at my work—at my soul laid bare on the page.

It's always like that. I don't know any other way to draw.

"And don't be afraid to use your eraser. Sometimes the absence of a mark can make the greater impact." He glances at me, green eyes searching, and I nod like an idiot. Always so tongue-tied around him. Always dizzied by his attention.

"Thanks, professor," I manage at last, my voice scraping out of my tight throat, and something flickers behind his eyes. He's so close still, leaning over my shoulder, that toned chest looming into my space—

Professor Reeve straightens up, and I can breathe again.

It's not a good trade.

His footsteps drum on the tiled floor as he strides away, head turning left and right as he examines the other students' work. His dark blond hair falls over his forehead, and though he's slender, his toned shoulders stretch his white button-down shirt.

I watch him go, my charcoal gripped uselessly in my hand, feeling kind of woozy on my wobbly stool. It's only when his sharp eyes land on me again that I jerk back to action.

Drawing. Still life.

Right.

My first swipes with the charcoal are messy. All wrong. I'm heavy-handed in my eagerness to show that I'm working, and now my ugly lines will take even longer to fix. I blow out a harsh sigh, frowning at the mess on my sketchpad, and force myself to concentrate.

Get it together.

He barely even knows you exist.

My next lines are better. More confident. And I shift my weight on the stool, feeling the quiet chatter of the classroom fade away. There's a part of me—one I'd rather not dwell on—that always knows where the professor is. That is hyper attuned to his footsteps on the tiles and his low murmur as he gives guidance, no matter how much I try to forget he's here.

Worst of all is hearing the giggles of the girls trying to flirt with him. Hearing their teasing words, their breathy calls for help.

I mean, I can't blame them. Maybe if I had the guts, I'd tease him like that too. But I'm not bold enough, and even though it's petty, I'd still rather stick pencils in my ears than listen to it.

Other than him, though, I can tune the world out. Push it all away and lose myself in my work.

So I roll my stiff neck, flex my fingers around my charcoal, and draw.

* * *

"Leona."

I still, hand raised, exhaling in short puffs of air. Oh god, where have I gone wrong now? My eyes rake over my sketch, over the sharp lines and soft smudges, but I don't see it. It's rough, of course, we only started it today, but it's...

Well. It's *good*.

"Yes, professor?" My tongue darts out, wetting my bottom lip. I'm thirsty, my mouth and throat dry, and how long have we been doing this?

Professor Reeve's voice is thick with amusement as he stands by my shoulder.

"Class ended, Leona. A while ago. I know you have this period free—" *How the hell does he know that?* "—but I'm afraid I need to clear up. The next class will be here soon."

"Oh." My legs wobble as I hop down off my stool, and a firm hand catches my elbow. He steadies me, then whips his hand away. "God. I'm so sorry. I get caught up sometimes—"

"I know you do."

He doesn't sound annoyed. He sounds... proud. And when I turn and look at Professor Reeve directly for the first time today, his green eyes are fierce with approval.

"I'll help you clear up," I offer weakly. "It'll be faster with two of us."

Professor Reeve hesitates—he can probably see the way my hands shake as I shove my things into my bag. But when I glance up at him he nods once, sharp.

"Yes. Alright, thank you."

His footsteps echo through the old chapel as he strides away.

The professor's movements are brisk. Efficient. He clears away the art supplies with the ease of someone who has done this a thousand times before and knows every inch of the classroom by heart. I hurry to help, folding easels and stacking sketchbooks, but I barely scratch the surface before it's already done.

The chapel is empty. Wrapped in shadows, except for the weak sunlight filtering through the jewel toned windows. Only the still life remains, ghostly and striking in the shaft of light.

"Should we…" I gesture awkwardly at the table.

"No. The next class will use it too."

"Okay." My fingers wind together. "Um."

This is the part where I should leave. Where I should say *goodbye* and *thanks* like a normal person, then get the hell out of this room. Professor Reeve is a dangerous man for me to be around. He makes me want to do things, to say things—*reckless* things—and the longer we're alone, the harder it is to resist.

I take a shuffling half-step forward.

"Leona," he warns.

Does he know? Surely he can't know what I'm considering—the way I want to throw my arms around his neck. The way I want to bury my face in the hollow of his throat and breathe in his spicy scent.

"I'll see you tomorrow in class," he tells me, voice firm, and my heart sinks in my chest.

The dismissal is clear. Has he wanted me gone this whole time? Oh god, it's so *humiliating*, and I need to go. Need to get out, away from his knowing gaze.

"Yes," I whisper, stumbling back. I hitch my bag higher, squeezing the strap. "I'm—I'm sorry. Um. Bye." His forehead creases as I back away, concern and something else filling his eyes, but I don't stick around.

It's bad enough already.

"Leona," Professor Reeve calls, but I've already turned on my heel. I hurry out of the classroom, my bag bouncing on my hip, my shoulder glancing off the door frame. He calls me again, voice louder, but I push into the crowds of students in the corridor, letting the current of people carry me off.

A few people glance at me, curiosity piqued by my flushed

cheeks and too-bright eyes, but I duck my head and push toward the exit.

Nothing happened.

That's what I tell myself, trying to soothe the nerves churning in my stomach.

I didn't do anything. I didn't say anything. Any tension between us—it's all in my head, anyway.

By tomorrow, Professor Reeve will have forgotten all about it.

* * *

I catch up with my roommate Avery by the art department notice board. She's leaning against the wall, reading something on her phone with a dreamy look on her face, and my nerves have calmed enough when I reach her for me to flick her on the shoulder.

"It's soppy, you know. How in love you are."

Avery shrugs, unapologetic. "Ellis texts me in between teaching his classes."

An ugly kind of envy slides through my stomach, and I force myself to smile. Avery got *her* professor crush. He loves her so fiercely, he risked everything to be with her, and now they're so heart-stoppingly in love, it hurts sometimes to be around.

It's a reminder.

I don't inspire that kind of passion. Not from the man I want.

"I suppose that's sweet," I admit to her, because I'm not a complete asshole. It's not Avery's fault that I'm jealous; that I have these small, ugly feelings inside me.

Avery smirks, eyes twinkling. "I wouldn't call this text *sweet...*"

"Stop right there." I hold up a palm. "My cold, dead heart can't handle it."

I'm joking—mostly—and Avery grins, but something over her shoulder catches my eye. It's a flier, pinned to the community cork board among the notes selling art supplies and begging for ride-shares out of town.

Life Models Wanted.

My skin flushes hot under my collar. We have regular life drawing classes here at college, drawing nudes in a series of poses, but the models are never *students.* They're always older adults from town, with brisk attitudes, who barely seem to notice that they're naked in front of a room full of strangers.

I've always kind of marveled at that. Those confident models seem so powerful.

A brief image flashes across my mind—modeling *here.* Taking my clothes off and feeling Professor Reeve's heavy gaze on my body. But when I scan the flyer quickly, that image fades as fast as it came.

The class is off campus. At a famous art studio in the city.

Still...

I chew on my bottom lip, reading the details over and over. It's well paid. It's a professional art studio—nothing seedy or weird. And it's for *art.*

The best part is in the small print at the bottom: *models may attend community classes free of charge.*

I tug the flier down before I can overthink it. The art studio in the city has equipment that we don't have here, and experts in weird and wonderful techniques. Professor Reeve and the other department staff are limited to the college curriculum, but the city studio...

The special classes I could take clamor in my brain.

And more than that—my heart still aches from Professor Reeve's dismissal. From being brushed off so abruptly.

I could use some power. Some confidence. Some take-no-shit attitude. Avery cranes her neck, reading the flier over my shoulder, and whistles softly.

I swallow hard. "What do you think?"

She huffs a laugh, nudging my shoulder with her own.

"I think it sounds badass."

Mason

The second the classroom door shuts behind Leona, I dig the heels of my palms into my eyes. My heart gallops in my chest, too fast to be healthy, and I let out a ragged groan.

The hurt in her expression. The way she stumbled back from me, so clumsy and eager to leave. The hitch in her voice.

Fuck.

I should never have kept her here with me alone.

When the bell rang in the hallway, signaling the end of class, all the other students heard it. They packed away their things, chatting among themselves, and filed around Leona's stool as she stayed there, lost in her work. Her long brown hair was piled up in a messy bun, her cheeks flushing with concentration, and there was a smudge of charcoal on the tip of her freckled nose.

Some of the other students nudged each other and pointed. Stifled their laughter as they wove between workstations to the exit.

But I heard it. I made a note of everyone who made fun

of Leona. They might think it's hilarious that she gets so absorbed in her art, but *I* know better.

She has talent.

True talent. And an artist's soul.

Something those idiots can only ever dream of.

That's why I let her stay. Why I gave into the voice whispering in my head, and sat back against a desk behind her. Not cleaning up, not marking assignments, just—watching. Watching her work.

We stayed there in silence for fifty minutes, and I don't think she realized once what was happening. She gnawed on her bottom lip, too tangled up in her drawing, and swept her charcoal across her sketchbook. The gentle rustle against the paper, over and over—that's all I could hear. That, and my thundering heart.

Once, about twenty minutes in, she paused to rub at her stiff shoulder. Her hand left charcoal fingerprints on her cream sweater, and I stood rigid against the desk as she let out a throaty moan. She tipped her head left and right, stretching her neck, a single dark curl dangling against her pale skin.

God, I want to hear that moan again.

I want her charcoal fingerprints all over me.

No. I shut the thought down—I've done more than enough damage today. It was reckless of me to let her stay here alone with me, knowing how unforgivable my thoughts are about Leona Ridley. What if I'd let slip? What if she'd glanced behind her by chance, and seen me staring at her like a cat watching a mouse?

She's my student. A gifted one.

But that must be all.

For a careful man, I am making so many reckless mistakes today. Seeing Leona's face crumple with hurt, seeing her flee from me into the corridor—it sets a restless energy pulsing under my skin. And I'm drawn through the art department corridors with a single-minded purpose, my feet carrying me with an unstoppable stride.

I shouldn't look. I shouldn't go in there, not during the daytime, when students mill everywhere and anyone could burst in without knocking.

But I do it. I prowl back to my office, practically snarling with frustration, and kick the door shut behind me. I toss my stack of notes and assignments onto the desk as I pass, crossing directly to the wooden door opposite—my storage cupboard.

Other professors keep office supplies in theirs. Stacks of post-it notes and boxes of pens. It looks innocent, with its plain wooden door and simple lock, and damn it, it *should* be innocent.

Instead, shame crowds my throat.

I draw the key out of my shirt, where it hangs on a cord against my bare chest. I can't risk anyone getting hold of it. I'm the only person on campus with access to this cupboard, and thank god, because if anyone saw its contents…

I'd be ruined.

The key slides into the lock. I glance over my shoulder, but the office door is shut. Holding my breath, I grip the key tight and spin it.

The cupboard door creaks as I pull it open, and I'm hit with a waft of dried paint and turpentine. A bare light bulb dangles from the ceiling, and I tug its cord, chest tight, as I step into the small space.

From every shelf, from every canvas, Leona stares back at me.

Her big brown eyes burn with every emotion I've ever seen pass over her face—humor. Passion. Sadness. Longing. She's so expressive, the emotion bleeding through her eyes, and each time I see a new one, I'm a man possessed.

I must paint it. Capture it. Document every shade of this girl who owns my soul. Leona has never simply been my student—from the first time I laid eyes on her, she became my muse. Even when I draw from other models at the studio in the city, it's *her* I see.

I only ever paint her above the shoulders. It's bad enough, this obsession, without letting myself run wild. If I were to let loose, if I allowed my gaze to linger on her perfect frame—the swell of her hips, her perky chest straining against those sweaters she wears—

"Fuck." I tug hard on the light cord, plunging myself into darkness. My breaths come loud and ragged, my skin too hot and tight.

I linger for a moment in the velvety shadows. Surrounded by the proof of my secret obsession.

I clear my throat. Shut my eyes and count to ten.

Then I step out of the cupboard, shut the door, and spin the key in the lock. My racing heartbeat only begins to calm once the key is safely back around my neck and I'm sat behind my desk, flicking through student sketchbooks. Bursts of laughter echo through my closed office door, the sounds of student life spilling through the cracks.

Leona belongs out there. In the laughter and sunshine.
Not in the darkness with me.

Leona

I stand on the sidewalk outside the *Graphite* art studio, staring up at the sign above the door. It's deep black, with sharp white lettering—so classy, so *grown up*. And here I am, with my skinny jeans and ankle boots and worn leather jacket. My hair falls in loose waves down my back, tugged by the wind, and I've tucked an old summer camp t-shirt into my waistband.

Crap.

I should have dressed smarter. Should have put on makeup and tried to look more mature. I thought about it too, my hand hovering over the makeup bag in my bedroom before I snatched it back and headed out, face bare.

I figured they'd rather I look natural. And that my clothes wouldn't matter, since I'd be taking them off anyway.

Oh god. Oh god, oh god.

What have I got myself into?

"Want me to come in with you?" My other roommate Paige stands by my side, peering up at the sign with a doubtful expression. She's wearing her ballet clothes beneath an enormous gray sweater which can only be her new boyfriend's. The huge folds of fabric swamp her, emphasizing her slender frame and making her look like a storybook elf with cold, pink ears.

Paige would make an amazing life model. She's elegant and slender, her muscles defined by years of ballet.

I glance down at my worn jeans and soft thighs and sigh.

Dignity is overrated anyway.

"No." I flash her a quick smile. "You'll be late for your dinner. Tell Raphael I say hi."

"Are you sure?" She hovers, worried, and that more than anything straightens my spine. This isn't something to get worked up over. It's not worth *stressing* about, and it's definitely not worth Paige missing her romantic dinner.

It's one evening. A humiliating evening, maybe, but then it'll be over and I can pretend it never happened.

"I'm sure." My smile is real this time. "Go on. Order something shamelessly cheesy for me."

"I will." She grins at me, fluttering a wave before taking off down the busy sidewalk. It's evening, the lamplights glowing to life overhead, and in the distance, a tall man with dark hair raises his arms as she approaches.

Of course. Raphael would never let Paige walk alone at night—he's too protective by far. I linger for a moment in the middle of the sidewalk, watching my friend get swept up against her lover's chest. Something pulses deep inside me—a horrible, lonely ache—and I cough once before stepping inside.

No point moping about on the sidewalk. And no time, anyway. I've got to take my shabby clothes off in front of fancy strangers.

* * *

"Lila! Good, you're here. Come along, we'll get you ready for the session."

The second I step through the doorway into the right studio, an older woman with braided silver hair sweeps me to one side. She's a whirlwind of energy, her mouth set in a no-nonsense line, and she tugs my jacket off my shoulders with brisk hands.

"I've got it," I mumble, ducking out of her grip. "And it's Leona."

Maybe I'm being rude, but she's knocked me off kilter. The woman's eyebrows shoot up her forehead, and I brace to get fired before I've even begun, but then she rolls her eyes and smiles.

"Oh dear. I'm doing it again, aren't I?"

Maybe? How should I know? I shrug, helpless, and the woman clicks her tongue, ushering me more slowly this time to a screen in the corner. I peer around the studio as we walk, but I don't have time to see much—just a dozen wooden easels, arranged in a loose circle around a space in the center of the floor. There's a plain foam mattress and a wooden chair in the center, and the first few artists are setting up their stations.

Oh god.

A mattress. A *mattress?*

"Don't worry, it's for any lying down poses. No funny business."

I whip my head around, forcing an awkward smile for the woman.

"Right. Yeah, no, of course."

Behind the screen, there's a rectangular mirror, a hook on

136

the wall, and a small stool. A plain white robe hangs from the hook, crisp and freshly pressed.

"My name is Fran." Her tone is clipped but warm, just like the rest of her as she nudges me further behind the screen. "I'm the studio owner, and I'll be running this session. Have you done this before, my dove?"

Leona, I want to tell her again, but I don't push it.

"No." I shake my head, and try to press my shoulders back. "But I can do it. Definitely."

Even if only for the free classes, I can do this. The whole confidence building thing… yeah, that's a lost cause.

"Good. Very good." She claps her hands together and rubs them, nodding at the robe. "Take your clothes off and leave all your things here. And when you're ready, come out in your robe."

"Okay," I mumble, but she's already gone, her voice booming as she greets the artists entering on the other side of the screen. This isn't a student class—a lot of the people here tonight are professionals.

Nerves flutter in my belly, but there's excitement too.

Maybe I can sneak a look at their work. Maybe I'll learn something useful, being on the other end of this process. Maybe, the next time Professor Reeve arranges a life drawing class for us, I could impress him. Show him something special.

No. I give myself a little shake. This isn't about Professor Reeve. This is about being brave, and getting closer to the art, and new opportunities. I make a mental list of everything I *should* be focused on, dragging my summer camp t-shirt over my head, and fold it before dropping it on the stool.

The hum of conversation grows louder beyond the screen as I quickly peel off my clothes. I move quickly, flicking open buttons and tugging down zippers. Kicking off my ankle boots. As I strip, cool air washes over my bare skin, pebbling my nipples, and god, what if they think I'm turned on?

I cinch the robe tight around my waist, peering down at the two points pushing against the fabric with dismay. This must happen to a lot of models. It *must*. It's cold in the studio, and nerves are buzzing under my skin, adrenaline surging through my veins.

Just a normal biological response. It's fine. It's *fine*. I give myself one final shake, then step out from behind the screen.

My nervous smile freezes on my face.

Professor Reeve stares at me from behind an easel. He's wide-eyed, the color draining from his face as I watch, and I open my mouth to say something. *Anything.*

A tiny little squeak comes out. Fran booms out a laugh, coming over to clap me on the shoulder.

"Be gentle with her, everyone! This is Leona's first time, isn't it, dove?"

My cheeks burn as I nod. She means modeling, obviously, but I can't help thinking of the other meaning. Especially with Professor Reeve's eyes burning into me, a muscle ticking in his clenched jaw. I've never done *that* before either, but I've thought about it plenty of times.

Thought about what it would be like—with *him*.

"I…"

I don't know what to say. I'm making such a fool of myself. Someone chuckles on the other side of the room and I glance around, cheeks burning, but there are only polite smiles and encouraging nods.

Professionals. These are professionals. I exhale slowly, pulse calming. And when Professor Reeve steps around his easel, eyes fixed on me, I don't even flinch as he moves closer. He's dressed more casually than on campus, in dark jeans and a black sweater, but he still looks kind of forbidding.

"May I have a word with Leona, Fran?" He asks her the question, but his eyes don't leave my face. And Fran stutters, taken aback, but waves him closer.

"Ah, yes! Of—of course, Mason."

Mason. So that's his first name. I wish I could say it out loud, trying out the feel of it in my mouth. But this is weird enough already, so I grit my teeth and wait for Professor Reeve to stop in front of me, ducking his head to murmur in my ear.

"Would you like me to leave, Leona? I can make an excuse. Just say the word—I don't want to make you uncomfortable."

I'm shaking my head before he's done talking. Do I want him to leave?

I never want that.

"No," I whisper. "You don't have to go. I don't mind."

Out of the corner of my eye, his hand twitches toward me. But he snatches it back, balling it into a fist and shoving it into his pocket.

"Please know, if I had realized you were modeling tonight… " He trails off. Like he's unsure what he would have done. Whether he would have stayed away.

The unspoken end of his sentence lingers between us.

"I'm glad you're here." I wet my lip, risking a glance up at him. He stares down at me, his chest so close, his eyes so green. "It's kind of nerve wracking. It's nice to know someone in the room."

His eyes shut for a long moment. He draws in a shuddering breath.

When he looks at me again, his pupils are blown wide.

"I'm going to draw you," he warns. "All of you." His gaze roams over my robe as he speaks, as though he's already planning his study. My nipples bead harder, a dull throb flaring between my legs. "If you don't want that, you must say so now. Last chance, Leona."

I squeeze two handfuls of robe, creasing the crisp fabric with my nervous hands.

"Stay." The word is quiet, but it lands between us like a ten ton weight. "Please, professor. I want you to stay."

* * *

I'm not often the center of attention. In classes or mixers, even out on the campus quad, I don't draw attention to myself.

I'm not shy, exactly. I'm reserved. When people pay attention to you, you have to guard your words. Watch how you behave. I much prefer to skip all that and bury my nose in a sketchbook.

There's no hiding now. No ducking out of sight. As I slide the robe's belt undone, every pair of eyes is fixed on me. It might have been overwhelming, but I keep my gaze locked on one person in particular.

His throat bobs when my robe drops to the floor.

"Wonderful!" Fran's sudden shout makes me jump, but she's beaming at me and I can't be annoyed. "That's the hardest part over with. Now, if you step into the center, we'll run through some quick fire poses."

I'm always grateful for these when I'm behind the easel. The series of fast poses, held only for a few seconds at a time, are a chance for the artists to loosen their wrists and warm their fingers. But now I realize they help the model too.

There's no time to die of embarrassment when I'm thinking up a new pose every few seconds. I can't even get self conscious about the way a certain pose makes my stomach look, or how knobbly my ankles are, because time is up and I'm moving on already.

With every new pose, I steal a glance at Professor Reeve. His easel is close, close enough for me to hear the whisper of his pencil over the page, and he draws with furious concentration. His eyebrows pull together and he glares at his page like it's annoyed him, and I swear, it's the most human he's ever seemed.

I know that feeling. When your mind is clear but your hand won't obey. And when our eyes finally clash, I offer a small smile.

Professor Reeve looks down, his jaw ticking again. And I move into a new pose, throat suddenly tight.

"Time to slow down." Fran nods at me, briskly approving, and I move to a simple standing pose. One I can hold for minutes at a time. I stand facing away from Professor Reeve, one hip jutted out, one arm draped over my head.

It feels kind of silly, but I can see myself in a distant mirror. I look *good*.

Like a real artist's model.

And since Professor Reeve has stopped smiling at me, I look at my reflection instead. My skin is pale, dusted with freckles, and my hip bones jut above soft thighs. I'm imperfect, nicked with old scars.

But seeing myself stood proud, nude in front of these strangers, basking in the glow of their attention...

Heat pools in my core.

A pricking sensation tells me my nipples are hardening again. I swallow, but this time, I'm not ashamed. My body is an artwork, a flawed masterpiece, and when I feel the telltale heaviness of Professor Reeve's gaze, I arch my back slightly.

His breath hitches.

Did anyone else hear that? Is anyone else tuned into this man like I am? There's only the rustle of paper, the scrape of pencils and charcoal. A cleared throat. The floor creaking beneath someone's shifted weight.

"Thank you, Leona. Let's move to the floor."

This is it. The lying pose. My newfound confidence falters as I scramble awkwardly onto the mattress, stretching out on the floor. It's impossible not to feel vulnerable down here, and I fidget when I should be still. Trying to get comfortable.

"Rest your head on your arm." It's Professor Reeve that speaks, his low, smooth voice reverberating through the studio. I huff quietly and do what he says, rolling over so that I'm staring right at him. My knees bend slightly, my hair splaying over the mattress, and he watches me with barely concealed hunger.

The ache throbs harder between my legs. I bite my lip and squeeze my thighs together, seeking secret relief.

Professor Reeve's mouth ticks up at the corner.

He *knows*. He knows about my ache. And he likes it.

Likes seeing me stretched out like an offering.

Maybe he's like this with other life models too, staring so intently their skin flushes hot all over. But no—the thought makes my stomach churn, even as I dismiss it.

I've seen him in life drawing class. He's never like this.

Tonight, Professor Reeve is not calm and contained.

142

Tonight, the primal energy that he hides so well… it's simmering just beneath the surface.

"Isn't she a peach?" Fran asks softly, and there are murmurs of agreement. I blink—I'd almost forgotten there were others here, that Professor Reeve and I weren't alone.

Alone.

My eyes glaze over as I picture it. Doing this, peeling my clothes off and stretching out for him to draw, but with no one else here. No one to dictate the poses.

No one to see what happens next.

"That's time! Thank you, Leona." Fran's clap makes me jump. The sounds of the studio fade back in—the quiet fumblings of the artists packing away their stations. I sit up awkwardly, suddenly keenly aware once again that I'm naked, and I take Fran's offered robe with eager hands.

The hour went so quickly. And I was barely aware, held spellbound by a pair of hungry green eyes.

Even once my robe is safely belted, my cheeks are still flushed.

"How was that?" Fran murmurs. "Not so terrible after all?" She smiles at me faintly, and she seems almost knowing. Like she could sense the tension crackling in the air between Professor Reeve and I.

"It was… interesting," I hedge. "To be on this side of the easel."

Fran nods, pleased. "An artist! Of course. Don't forget your free class, dove."

"I won't." We chat for a minute longer, until someone else distracts her and I can slip away back to my clothes.

It's weird getting dressed. Like I was more myself, somehow, for the last hour, and now I'm getting ready to play-act as someone else. My clothes fit, obviously, but they don't seem to hang properly when I pull them back on. I fasten my ankle boots with clumsy fingers.

I can't have taken more than two minutes to dress. I'm too eager to return to the warm glow of Professor Reeve's attention, to try for a glimpse at his drawing of me. But when I step back out from behind the screen, tugging my leather jacket over my shoulders, his easel stands empty.

He's gone.

Mason

What the fuck was I thinking? I should have left Graphite the second I saw Leona there with her bare toes poking out from under that white robe. The first glimpse I got of her peering around the screen, I thought I was hallucinating. That my dark obsession with my innocent student had finally driven me insane.

But no. She was there. It was really her.

And I saw all of her.

I may not have painted Leona below the neck before, but I've imagined her body more times than I can count. While my attention wanders behind my desk; while biting my knuckles in the shower; late at night when I toss and turn in my bed.

I've always known she'd be gorgeous. It doesn't take an artist to see that. No one could have such soft freckled skin, such expressive brown eyes, and not be mouthwatering all over.

But god. After seeing her properly...

I'm wrecked.

"Fuck." My strides eat up the sidewalk, lamplight bouncing

off the dark puddles of rainwater. It must have stormed while we were inside—how appropriate. Now I'm the one tossed on hurricane winds.

My canvas is tucked below my arm, wedged tight against my side like someone might snatch it away. I'd planned on using paper, on just practicing tonight, but the second I saw it was Leona, I switched out to canvas.

She is a sight I want to remember.

"Asshole," I mutter to myself, and a woman waiting at a bus stop shuffles away from me as I storm past. My apartment is not far from here, only a few blocks' walk, and at this rate, I'll burst through the doors in record time. The restless energy that I always feel around Leona—it's surging under my skin again. But tonight, after seeing her laid out bare in front of me, after seeing her wet her lips and stare at me with such longing—

Fuck.

I should never have stayed. There's no way I'll be able to keep away now.

Briefly, I consider turning in my resignation. I like working as an art professor well enough, but over the last few years I've become a well known painter in my own right. I've garnered enough acclaim that I could quit the college and live off my art, never having to torment myself with Leona's big eyes or her delicate scent again.

I could do it.

I could leave.

I *could*, goddamn it.

So why am I dismissing the idea without real consideration?

A scowl twists my normally calm face as I pound up the stone steps to my apartment entrance. I live in a pale stone town house, chosen for its nearness to the city's art district, its elegant wrought iron balconies, and high, arching ceilings. The doorman nods at me as I brush past, then does a double take, but I don't stop after muttering a greeting.

I'm not fit for society right now.

I clutch my canvas tighter.

The elevator doors stand open, ready to whisk me up to my top floor apartment. But I'm still wound too tight, grinding my teeth so hard they might crack, so I plunge into the stairwell instead, pounding up three steps at a time.

My chest is heaving when I push through my front door, but not from exertion. Not really. I'm unraveling now that I'm safely out of sight, coming apart at the seams. Pushed beyond my breaking point by the sight of Leona's body, stretched out on the mattress, her wrist draped over the swell of her hip.

Those dusky pink nipples, beading against the cool studio air.

I wanted to lick them. I wanted to toss my pencil down, round my easel, drop into a crouch beside her, and run the flat of my tongue across her chest.

God, even now...

I need her.

I take care to place the canvas on a table. Flick a single lamp on, bathing myself in its glow. Then I tear at my button with rigid fingers, drawing my hard cock out of my jeans. It's flushed an angry red, swollen harder than I've ever been, and I hiss between my teeth as I give it a tug.

Leona would be gentle. Teasing. So I'm the opposite: gripping myself too hard, jerking too fast. I'm rough and punishing, and it's no more than I deserve, especially when I bite down on my fist and unleash a ragged groan. Her wide eyes were so trusting, so grateful that I was near, to provide *support*, not to imagine myself pressing her thighs apart and fucking her right there in front of everyone.

A devious thought flashes across my mind: the artists standing around us with their easels, watching calmly as I fuck Leona into a quivering heap. Raising their pencils to get the proportions right, sketching quietly behind her moans.

Because I would make her moan.

Count on that.

My cock jerks in my hand and I squeeze harder, pump faster, until my teeth dig into the skin of my hand and my balls draw up tight. I tense, holding my breath as I come so hard, white spots float before my eyes.

Drops rain hot over my fingers.

Fuck, I want that on *her*. Painting the bare skin of her stomach.

"Asshole." The reminder is too late. I'm slumped against the wall, my clothes rucked and my hair wild.

I already saw Leona.

And I can never go back.

* * *

Part of me thought she might be embarrassed. That once the spell woven by the art studio wore off, Leona would regret showing herself to me like that and might transfer to another class.

But when I unlock the old chapel for the morning's first session, a soft voice rings out behind me.

"Hi, Professor Reeve."

I pause. My grip tightens on the brass door handle, the metal creaking and growing warm.

"Hello, Leona."

I don't turn back. I don't trust myself, not out here in the corridor where anyone could walk past and see the wild glint in my eyes. The door creaks on its hinges as it swings open, the classroom inside cool and quiet.

Our footsteps echo off the stone tile floors. At the sinks lining one wall, a faucet drips.

"Did you enjoy the class?"

I choke back a laugh. Did I enjoy it, having my world shaken upside down?

"Yes." I stride to the still life set up on a center table, prodding at a fold of tablecloth. Someone has changed the display.

"Are you—um. Are you angry with me?" She asks it so timidly, her voice small where she stands by the entrance. Leona has barely stepped inside the classroom, hanging back while I avoid her eye, and I can't hold off any longer.

I turn to her.

Leona sucks in a sharp breath, her eyes growing wide. Her arms are wrapped around her slender waist, her hands disappearing into her open jacket, but as I watch, her arms tighten and squeeze.

"Angry?" My voice is as soft as I can manage. I prowl towards her, my hands tucked in my pockets. "Why would I be angry?"

A burst of laughter echoes down the corridor outside, and I grimace, reaching over Leona's shoulder to shove the door closed. The thud echoes through the silence, fading slowly until it's just us—our breaths, our rapid heartbeats. Leona's pulse taps against the side of her throat.

I want to scrape my teeth over it.

Leona gathers herself, asking her next question with effort. "If you're not angry, why are you…" She trails off, unwrapping one arm to gesture vaguely at the tense set to my shoulders.

"It's not anger." I crowd closer, so close that she has to tip her chin back to hold my eye. "It's…" I search for the right word. One that will explain my mood without shocking her. *Soul-deep desperation* doesn't seem to cut it. "It's discomfort." I arrange my face into a smile. "I acted poorly yesterday. I should not have stayed."

"But… you said you enjoyed it…"

God, is that hurt in her eyes? Is it *shame*? I can't bear it.

"Yes. That's—that's the problem. I enjoyed it too much, Leona."

She frowns slightly, her smooth forehead puckering, then understanding dawns. And it's like watching the sun break over the horizon, warmth and light cresting over her face.

She sways closer to me. I don't think she even realizes it. But now her puffed breaths waft over my bare throat.

"I liked it too." Her eyes drop to my mouth briefly. My heart drums louder, lunging against my ribcage. "Modeling felt…"

She trails off. If I don't hear the end of that sentence, I will go insane.

"How did it feel?" I urge.

"Powerful." The word bursts out of her, seems to take her by surprise. Her tongue darts out to wet her plump bottom lip. "Feeling everyone's eyes on me—feeling *your* eyes on me—"

A growl escapes my throat.

It's reckless. So foolish, and yet if I don't taste her this second, my heart will beat clean through my chest. I plunge my hands into her hair, gripping the sides of her face, and draw her lips up to mine.

Leona moans, her hands fisting in my shirt. She bows, arching her body against me, sealing us together from head to toe. I've never stopped to consider how this would feel—her weight and warmth pressed against me. But it's so perfect, so right, like slotting puzzle pieces together, and I never want her to step away from me again.

Sharp teeth dig into my lip, and blood surges to my cock. I want her *now*, I want her breathless, I want her spread open and moaning—

The door rattles on its hinges, a muffled thump the only warning we get before the brass door handle twists. Leona leaps back, breathing hard, two spots of color burning high on her cheeks, and I only have time to grind out her name before the classroom door swings open.

"Morning, professor!"

This cheery student will be the death of me. I grunt in greeting, too far gone to string sentences together. Whoever it is doesn't seem to notice, chattering away about today's session, and Leona shoots me a small, dazed smile before stepping around me.

I stare at the wall as her footsteps echo to her easel.

This class will be torture.

* * *

Still life. Fucking *still life*.

Who cares about a table of underripe fruit when Leona Ridley is *right there*? If there were any true artists in this room besides her, they would spin their easels around and draw her instead. But no—I have to stroll between workstations, giving pointers on how to capture the texture of orange peel.

Idiots.

Every now and then, I feel her gaze on me. I *feel* it, like a fingertip running down my spine. And when I glance over, she's turned my way, mouth curled in amusement.

My frustration must be etched all over my being.

"Is that a satsuma or a tangerine?" one girl asks, the end of her pencil chewed between her teeth.

"Does it matter?" I snap. Leona sinks lower on her stool, her shoulders shaking.

"Well, maybe…"

I scrub a hand over my face. "Only if you plan to eat it."

The class is eternal. Stars are born and continents shift as I prowl between easels, straining to hear the bell.

When it finally rings through the corridors, echoing and shrill, I sag in relief.

"Good class, everyone. Leona—a word, please."

No one raises an eyebrow. They all know how serious Leona is about her art; it's not unusual for her to linger with questions.

Now it's my turn to keep her here. To savor her, just for a few minutes longer.

"Congratulations." She sidles up to me beside the still life display as the last two students shuffle through the doorway. The door bangs shut behind them, and we're alone. "You seemed almost normal for that class."

I grip her shoulders and spin her round, caging her in against the table. "Only almost?"

Leona shrugs one shoulder. I'd think she was unaffected if

her breaths weren't coming so fast. "You got kind of worked up about fruit at the end."

My smile is vicious. And fuck, I wanted to hide this from her. My rough edges; my wildest urges. But she doesn't flinch away—she tilts her head to give me better access as I lick a stripe up her neck.

"Can you blame me?" I breathe in her ear. Pressing forward, my body flattens against hers, and there's no way she could mistake the hard length of my cock digging into her stomach. "I finally get to taste you, then I have to keep my distance for a whole hour."

"Fifty minutes," Leona gasps as I suck on the skin beneath her ear, rocking my hips against hers. She grips my elbows, tugging me closer. "The class is fifty minutes."

"Well it felt like a hundred years," I say flatly, moving to the other side of her neck. She tilts her head again, her hair whispering over her shoulders.

I lean back, jolted by the sight of her t-shirt. The faded purple cotton with the cracked summer camp logo.

"You wore this yesterday." I pluck at her shoulder. "I saw it on the stool by the screen."

She shrugs, cheeks flaming. Suddenly stiff and embarrassed.

"It's clean," she clips out. "I only wore it for two hours."

Does she think I'm complaining? Hardly. I only noticed because I've been obsessing over this t-shirt. *I* want to be the one to take it off her. To drag it slowly over her arms, baring her inch by perfect inch, then drop it to the ground, the fabric still warm from her body.

"I like it." I capture her mouth with mine, inhaling deeply as we kiss. Our mouths are closed, but already I'm lost. Under her spell. And when Leona's lips part, when her tongue shyly brushes mine, I could shatter the wooden table with my bare hands.

There are noises in the corridor. The sounds of college life. Students talking loudly as they move between classes; the clatter of footprints and the slamming of doors. There's no class in here for this period, but that doesn't mean no one will come in. The door is unlocked, and the supplies here are free for students to use.

None of that matters. I grip Leona by the waist and lift her onto the table. The tablecloth rucks up, an apple rolling onto the floor, but she whimpers, dragging me by the shirt to stand between her spread legs.

"You're going to come for me." I smooth my palms up her thighs, the fabric of her jeans whispering under my touch. "I *will* hear you come."

I'm being such a caveman, practically rubbing my scent all over her to stake a claim, but I don't care. And judging by the flush spreading down her throat, neither does she.

"P-Professor Reeve—"

"Mason."

"Mason, I'm... I've never done this before."

My forehead drops onto her shoulder. I breathe in hard through my nose, willing the blood roaring in my ears to ease off for a moment.

"Would you like to stop?" I manage.

"No." She sounds horrified. "No, I'm just—I don't want you to be disappointed."

"Impossible." I straighten up and fix her a glare. I need her to see how serious I am. "You could never disappoint me. Not when you feel like *this*," I rock my hips against her core, groaning, "and taste like *this*." I descend on her again, plunging my tongue past those sweet lips. She melts, goes boneless and panting in my arms, and I flick her jeans button open.

Her zipper scrapes down, the sound loud in the old chapel.

"Stop me," I rasp. "Leona. Stop me."

"No." She grabs my wrist, guiding my hand inside her jeans. And she holds me there, as my fingers slide into her panties. As they nudge past soft lace and find her soaking core.

As if I could draw my hand back now.

As if I could stop this once we'd started.

I circle her clit, my grin savage when she whimpers. Leona's hips rock, restless on the table, as I explore the length of her seam, dipping in to rub at her entrance. And when I finally plunge two fingers inside her, crooking my knuckles to rub her walls, she tips her head back and *groans.*

"Do you like that, sweet girl?" I rock my hips against her, mindlessly seeking friction. I'm so hard I can feel it in my teeth. "Does it feel good when I stretch you?"

"Uh-huh." She nods, her reply a hiccup. *"More."*

I don't need to be told twice. I work a third finger inside her, circling her clit with my thumb. It's awkward, the angle clumsy and my hand catching on her jeans, but it's *perfect.* Especially when she clings to my shoulders, her whole body shaking.

"I... I..."

I press my bared teeth against her temple. Her hairline is damp, her body overheating. *"Yes.* Let it happen."

I work her steadily, ignoring the cramping muscles of my hand. Ignoring my neglected cock. Nothing matters except the tremor in her thighs; the wetness spreading beneath my fingers. And when Leona's breath catches, her body going rigid, a strangled moan leaving her mouth, I bite down on her shoulder and rub her until she slumps back, panting.

"God." Her words sound thick in her mouth. "Oh my god. That was—I think I heard colors."

I chuckle, inordinately pleased. And my heart swells, thundering as she reaches for me and runs a trembling hand along the outline of my cock.

Bang.

A nearby door slams outside, jerking us back to earth. We're still surrounded, still on the verge of being exposed, and there would be no explanation for how we're clasped together. For our flushed cheeks and the wreckage of the still life display behind Leona. The tablecloth is twisted, the fruit bowl knocked askew, and water has sloshed over the rim of the jug and soaked the table.

"You'd better go to class." I've never resented a sentence so much. But I press my mouth in a line, refastening her jeans quickly.

"Okay," she mumbles, and there's something behind those chocolate brown eyes. A sliver of doubt? "Will we—can I see you again?"

A rueful laugh bursts out of me, and a fond smile curls my mouth. I tuck a lock of hair behind her ear, rubbing her earlobe gently.

"I couldn't stay away now if I tried," I admit. "And what's worse, what is truly damning—I'm not going to." She beams up at me, so relieved, and I kiss her quickly before lifting her down. Her boots tap against the stone tiles. "Come back this evening. When classes are finished. Promise me, Leona."

I'll tear out my hair if she won't.

But she bites her lip and nods, smoothing her clothes before wandering toward the exit.

"See you later, professor," she calls softly from the doorway. The door clicks shut behind her.

I curse and press down hard on my cock, willing the pain to chase the arousal away.

Later. I'll see her later.

And the next time, I won't let her go.

Leona

"Oh my god." Avery checks the surrounding tables at the campus coffee shop, then leans in closer. All around us is the buzz of conversation, the clink of china, the hiss of steam. "Right there? In the classroom?"

I nod, my face numb.

It did happen, right? I didn't just hallucinate it out of sheer longing? Because *that* would be humiliating. Really, a new low.

"I am ninety-nine percent sure that it really happened and I didn't just drink some bad apple juice."

Avery wrinkles her nose, shaking her head as she sits back. "That's gross. No, it definitely happened."

I scan my friend's face for signs of judgment, but honestly, she looks kind of proud. Avery's blonde hair is scraped back in her trademark French braids, and her blue eyes sparkle as she tilts her head.

"Was it as good as you imagined?"

Avery knows how long I've been crushing on Professor

Reeve. I confessed soon after she landed her own hot professor. But I never dreamed that it might happen for me too—that I would feel his touch. Feel his warmth burning through my clothes. Breathe his masculine scent into my lungs.

"It was…" I search for the words. But they don't exist—there's no way to properly convey how it felt. Maybe if I had a few hours alone with my sketchbook, I could *draw* how I feel, but words… they're not my strong suit. "It was incredible," I settle for, even though that's the world's biggest understatement. "I never knew I could come like that."

Avery whistles long and low, eyes crinkling with amusement, but before she can tease me for *that* confession, a girl spins around at a neighboring table.

"Well, that makes sense," she blurts, looking between us. "This professor must be older, right? So he knows what he's doing."

My mouth drops open. I shoot a panicked look at Avery and find her staring back at me in horror. We thought it would be safe talking here, drowned out by other people's conversations, but this girl clearly heard every word.

The stranger raises her eyebrows. She's beautiful, with long platinum blonde hair and painted emerald nails. She's dressed more formally than the other students, in a white button down blouse and a pencil skirt—though a pair of sneakers are crossed under her chair.

"I'm Charlotte," she offers when we say nothing. "I work in the Dean's office."

"Hi," I manage at last, after unsticking my tongue from the roof of my mouth. "I'm Leona. This is Avery. I, uh… Listen, what you just heard—"

"Don't worry about it." Charlotte flaps a hand. "I'm just an admin girl. Unless you *want* me to report it, it's none of my business."

"And yet you were eavesdropping," Avery says drily. I kick her ankle under the table—the last thing we need to do is offend this girl. But Charlotte grins, pushing to her feet and swinging her chair around to our table.

"Yeah. Sorry about that," she says cheerfully, not sounding sorry one bit. "The Dean always shuts the door for the scandalous meetings. I don't get to hear any good gossip."

I don't really want what happened with Mason to be labeled as *gossip*. Sure, it would cause a scandal if it got out, but it wasn't seedy.

It was real.

"I'm not sure—"

"I know." Charlotte slaps her palm down on the table. "I'll give you some dirt on me, too. Then we're even, and we *have* to trust each other." I open my mouth to argue, but her face falls. "I don't have any friends here," she admits quietly. "I moved here three weeks ago. The only person who talks to me is the Dean, and that's only because he's my dad's best friend."

Crap. I'm a sucker for a sob story. I can't hear sad things and not be affected—it's why I read romance novels. I need that damn 'happily ever after', or it ruins my day.

"What's your dirt?" Avery asks, and she's softened too. When Charlotte glances over, she offers a small smile.

"Well." Our new friend blows out her cheeks, eyes going wide as she strains to think. Then a mischievous light comes over her, and she smirks. "I've got one. I've been hiding the Dean's ties. He takes them off when he goes running at lunch, and I've been stealing them from his bag and hiding them around the office."

But…

"*Why?*" Avery asks, as baffled as I am.

Charlotte shrugs. "He looks better without them." A dreamy look filters over her face. "When he can't find them, he undoes the top two buttons on his shirt."

Oh, wow. Talk about dirt. This girl could lose her job if we spread that around. But she's right—it's impossible not to trust each other now. A bond has been formed.

"So tell me about this professor." She scoots closer, resting her elbow on the table. "Is he hot?"

* * *

I've never felt a day drag so much in my life. I teased Professor Reeve—Mason—for being so impatient in class, but I get it now. I do. Waiting around on campus for classes to end, watching the other students wander the stone paths so *freaking slowly*…

It's torture.

It wasn't so bad earlier in the day, when I had my own classes to distract me. But by 3pm, my schedule is finished, and I still have three more hours to kill.

Three hours of brushing my mouth with my fingertips, remembering the way his lips slanted against mine. The scrape of his stubble on my cheeks; the decadent slide of his tongue.

Three hours of seeing his scorching stare every time I close my eyes, watching me so greedily, with such all consuming *hunger.*

Three hours of hearing the ragged groan that tore from his

chest the first time he kissed me.

Oh, god. I'll never make it through the day.

By early evening, I find myself in the library. There's nowhere else on campus that you can just *linger*, like a poltergeist, and no one bats an eye. Besides, endlessly wandering the stacks gives me a chance to burn off some of this restless energy.

My muscles are primed. My teeth are gritted, my heart pumping fast. My body is preparing for fight or flight, like there's a chance in hell that I'd do either when it comes to Professor Mason Reeve.

I want him. God, I want him so badly. My fingers tremble as I stroke along the book spines.

Has he done this before?

The unwelcome thought makes my stomach clench. And I feel weirdly guilty for even wondering it, like I'm betraying his trust by thinking poorly of him. It's not that I actually suspect him—Lord knows I've never seen him look at another student the way he looks at me. I just…

I want this to be special.

Special enough to risk his career over. Special enough to *last*.

I'll ask him. The minute I see him, I'll push my shoulders back and I'll ask him. And if he's angry with me for even thinking it, well… maybe he'll be firm with me. Maybe he'll let out some of that bottled up intensity.

I'd like that.

The sky outside the library windows fades to dusk, soft pinks and navy blues mingling above the clouds. The silence thickens between the stacks, like there are fewer people breathing here than there were an hour ago.

I pause between two bookshelves. Check left and right, then slide my hand under my t-shirt, stroking over my bare stomach. My nerve endings are so sensitive, I choke back a whimper, moving higher to palm my aching breast.

A door slams in the distance, and I whip my hand back out.

I'll wait. I'll wait for Mason.

Besides.

It's nearly time.

***

My ankle boots clip against the stone path as I hurry back to the art department. The campus street lamps are on, glowing orange against the dark sky, and the cool wind makes me shiver. I'd planned to be suave about this part. Strolling back casually, not a care in the world.

But now that the moment is here, I'm almost running, my breaths coming in quick pants.

The art department lobby is empty except for one girl leaning against the wall. She's clearly waiting for someone, yawning and checking her phone, and I smile awkwardly as I walk past. Further down the corridor, voices echo, and footsteps crunch past on the paths outside.

We're not alone. We never will be here. There will always be people around—always the risk of being caught.

That should *not* send heat pulsing through my core.

I'm going straight to hell.

The old chapel is attached to the main building, deep inside the warren of corridors. As I march along the tiles, the lights get dimmer. The distant voices fade. And when I finally grip the brass door handle to the chapel, my slamming heartbeat is the loudest sound.

"Leona." Professor Reeve stands in the center of the room, his hands in his pockets. "You came."

His dark blond hair is mussed, like he's been dragging his hands through it, and there's a glint in his eyes. Today, he's wearing dark pants and a white shirt rolled to the elbows, with a fitted vest that emphasizes his broad shoulders and nipped in waist. My mouth goes dry just looking at him.

"Leona," he repeats softly. "Come inside."

My feet get the memo before the rest of me, jolting to life and carrying me through the doorway. I shut the door behind me, but there's no key in the lock.

We'll have to take our chances.

When I turn back to Mason, his expression is unreadable.

"You can change your mind, you know." He cocks his head, watching me closely. "We can forget any of this ever happened."

A strangled laugh bursts out of me. "Maybe *you* can."

He smiles finally, though it does nothing to dull the sharpness of his face. Professor Reeve… he's kind of feral.

I'm halfway across the old chapel before I notice what's behind him. In the center of the room, in the shaft of light beaming from up in the rafters, there's a plain foam mattress. Just like in Graphite. Rather than a circle of easels, there's just one, with a blank canvas already set up.

Mason shrugs. "I couldn't resist. Drawing you in Graphite… " He breaks off and scrubs a hand over his face. When he speaks again, his voice is gravel. "You were perfect. Better than I'd ever dreamed."

164

It's the first time he's mentioned wanting me before, but of *course* he did. It's right there in his face. Months, maybe even years' worth of longing, harsh on his classically handsome features.

"You don't have to," he says again, and when will he stop trying to give me an out? I'm not running. I'm not changing my mind.

I want this.

I want *him*.

"What will you use?" I ask, shrugging off my leather jacket and tossing it onto a chair. Slowly, I tease my t-shirt out of my jeans waistband. His eyes drop, locking onto my hands as they grip my hem.

"Charcoal."

I hum, starting to draw my shirt up my stomach. "That's my favorite, too."

He's in front of me before I can blink, one hand wrapped around my wrist. His chest heaves as he rasps: "Let me."

I force my fingers to work. Drop my hem and raise my arms overhead.

The fabric is warm as it whispers past my face.

"I wanted to do this earlier," he confesses once my t-shirt is in his hands. He weighs it in his palm, thumb rubbing over the cotton, then abruptly lifts it to his nose and breathes in deep.

A bolt of heat shocks through my core.

He's so *primal*. Scenting me like an animal, even as his eyes roam over my newly bared skin. I fight to keep from crossing my arms over my chest. I'm not embarrassed of my body, but I never dreamed this could actually happen. If I had, maybe I'd have dressed in a nicer bra. A more sophisticated one, a padded black one with lace—not the simple white cotton one

I'm wearing.

"Fuck," Mason breathes, reaching out and brushing the backs of his knuckles over my stomach. My muscles clench, shuddering under the sudden contact, and I squeeze my thighs tighter.

"Professor." I scrabble at my jeans button. I can't take the teasing anymore. "Please."

Mason straightens, his face going blank. "Strip." The command echoes through the old chapel. "And lie down."

Taking off my clothes in Graphite was weird, but at least I had the screen. It was more like getting changed in a swimming pool cubicle than anything. Here, the professor watches my every move, his quick eyes cataloging everything I take off.

My ankle boots—kicked beneath a nearby table.

My socks. My jeans.

My bra.

I hesitate with my thumbs hooked in my panties, bare toes curling on the cold stone tiles.

"Last chance, Leona," he tells me softly.

I pull them down.

Hearing that sharp hitch in his breath—it buoys me. Swells my chest and raises my chin. I remember now what made Graphite so dreamlike. How *powerful* it felt. And when I stroll past Mason to the foam mattress, I add an extra swing to my hips.

"Jesus Christ," I hear him mutter, and I hide my smile as I turn and stretch out on the floor.

No warm up poses tonight. No quick-moving series.

We've waited long enough.

His steps drum against the floor. He's circling me. Staring.

"Roll onto your right side." I do as he says, tipping so that I'm facing his easel. He prowls behind me, still talking though I can't see his face. "Bend your knee."

I draw my left knee up slowly, waiting for him to say *when*. And a shocked gasp escapes me as warm hands grip me, guiding me into place. He's firm, exacting, arranging me like a doll until he's finally satisfied.

"Perfect." Mason sounds pained. I don't dare turn my head to look at him in case I ruin the pose he's made. But when he strides back into view, I bite down hard on my lip.

He looks wrecked. The professor is hanging by a thread.

I want that thread to snap.

The first sweeps of the charcoal are relaxed. Loose lines, meant to sketch the very barest outline. But as he settles into his work, his eyebrows drawing together, I feel his full focus. His gaze roams over my body, settling here and there, and not an inch of me goes unexamined. Every freckle, every dip and hollow, every soft bit that makes me blush—he is ravenous for it.

He doesn't say a word. He is silent, almost forbidding, as he scowls at his canvas, his shirt and vest so proper while I stretch out completely bare. And basking in the unrelenting glow of his attention, the pulse between my legs grows.

My breasts become heavy. Aching to be touched, with tight nipples beading against the air.

My hot skin is fevered, never mind the cool chapel, and every whisper of movement in the air makes me want to squirm.

The throbbing in my core is a pulse of its own. Urgent and needy.

"Mason," I whisper when I can't bear it any more. Sweat breaks out around my hairline; my thighs clench and press, the pose almost forgotten. And he takes one look at my pained expression, then tosses his lump of charcoal down.

"Forgive me." He strides around his easel and comes to crouch at my side. "I got lost in the sight of you."

His fingertips are stained black with charcoal. He reaches for my waist, then pauses, his hand hovering over my skin.

"I can clean up—"

"Don't." I suck in a shaky breath. "I want your handprints on me."

The groan rattles out of him, then I'm flipped onto my back. He smooths his hands up my stomach, drawing two faint lines, then squeezes my breasts, weighing them in both palms. He twists my nipples, just the right side of rough, and a dark smile tugs his mouth as I mewl beneath him.

"You're wound tight, aren't you, darling?"

I nod, arching my chest, pushing myself harder into his grip. He grunts, pleased, and smacks the tip of one breast. The sting—it makes my heart *soar*.

"I'll fix it," he grinds out, moving to kneel between my thrashing legs. "I'll make that ache go away."

A glance down my body makes my breath catch. Smeared fingerprints cover my breasts and stomach; they trace his path down to grip my hips. Mason squeezes me there too before taking hold of my thighs and spreading me wide.

Two days ago, I'd never been naked in front of a man.

Today, my professor is seeing every inch.

And he likes what he sees, judging by the starving glint in his eyes. By the snarl that tears out of him when my legs twitch closed, and he presses wide again and pins me there.

"No hiding yourself now." His chest heaves beneath his clothes. He's still fully dressed, so formal, so proper. But his hair is wild, falling over his forehead, and the hard line of his cock juts against his dark pants.

"Please." I don't know what else to say. Don't even know what I'm asking for. Only that he's the one person who can give it. "Professor Reeve. *Please.*"

His hand twitches towards my core, then he remembers the charcoal on his fingertips. He shoots me a rueful smile, before shifting back quickly and ducking his head.

The first swipe of his tongue—it's hot. Wet. So decadent and depraved that I cry out, bucking beneath him. Professor Reeve holds my thighs down with an iron grip, feasting on every inch of my pussy. The tip of his nose nudges my clit and I jerk, thumping my head against the floor.

"Careful," he grinds out, his words vibrating through my flesh, and that just makes it *worse.* I cry out, loud and long, as he licks me into the ground. As he renders me boneless and quivering.

"You're going to give us away." He's darkly amused, raising his head and looming above me. His chin is slick, his pupils blown wide. "We can't have that."

He crawls up my body before I can ask what he means. What he plans to do with me. And his belt buckle clinks as he works it free.

"Are you going to let me inside, Leona?"

I'm already nodding, the movement dizzying. "Yes. Yes."

Brutal satisfaction spreads over his face. "*Good.*"

He's swift. Rough. One minute he's leaning over me, drawing his hard cock from his pants. The next, the head is notched at my entrance, and he thrusts the first inches inside with a groan.

"Can't go too far," he pants in my ear, talking half to himself.

"Can't hurt your innocent pussy." His hips flex as he mutters, working himself in and out, giving me time to adjust. And it's a lot, it's a stretch, but I'm so soaking wet that he easily glides deeper inside me.

"Oh my *god*." I bow up off the mattress, biting down on his shirt-covered shoulder. Mason laughs, darkly thrilled, and thrusts deeper, harder, until we're sealed together and I'm crushed to the floor.

The weight of him. Being trapped by his bulk. The stretch of him lodged inside me.

I *love* it.

Sure, I can't breathe too well, but breathing is overrated, and when he lifts himself up slightly, I grumble in complaint.

"More. Mason, *more*."

He nips my chin, slamming his hips into mine. The professor sets a steady rhythm—not frantic. Assured. He pounds me into the mattress, his muscles bunching beneath his clothes, a droplet of sweat landing on my cheek. And I wrap my legs around his waist, hooking my ankles together, urging him deeper, trapping him there.

I never want this feeling to stop.

I feel so full. So right. So *alive*.

This time, when I can't hold back my cries, he seals his mouth to mine and swallows my moans. Mason adjusts his angle, rubbing harder along my walls, and my breath stops. I see *stars*.

"Oh my god," I tear my face away and mumble into his throat, my voice thick. "I'm—I'm going to—"

A slam echoes down the corridor, footsteps drumming closer. The sound filters into my awareness, but I'm too far gone to care. If he stops now, I'll die.

"You're mine," Mason growls, fucking me so hard my toes curl. He licks a stripe up my throat. *"Mine."*

I open my mouth to reply, to tell him yes, of course I'm his, but someone else speaks before me. The old chapel door swings open, groaning on its hinges, and a woman strides inside, her heels clicking on the stone tiles.

"Professor Reeve, I—"

Her footsteps stumble to a halt. She sucks in a horrified breath. And the image of what she's seeing—my older professor, fully clothed and snarling, pounding my smaller, bare body into the mattress—it ripples through me, molten in my veins.

"Fuck—Leona." Mason begins to pull out, already trying to cover my nakedness, but I hitch my ankles tighter, urging him back inside me again. "Oh, *fuck.*"

If I thought he was barely restrained before...

He's come undone.

Mason plants one hand on either side of my head, and slams his cock deep inside me. He fucks me fast and brutal, his top lip curled up in a snarl, and I barely even register the woman's retreating steps or the slam of the door.

"Don't. Stop." I pant between gritted teeth.

He bellows, ducking his head and sucking my nipple into his mouth. That sudden tug, the harsh, wet heat—

I detonate.

Wave after wave of pleasure wracks my frame, so much that tears brim in my eyes. It's too much, too good, and when Mason wedges himself deep inside me and spills, flooding me with warmth—I cry out.

We slump. Sweat cools on my bare skin, and Professor Reeve hangs his head above me. His shoulders heave with every breath, both of us gasping for air, and I want to reach for him but I can't move my limbs.

The press of his lips is gentle on my forehead. We both wince as he pulls out.

"I'm sorry," he says at last, voice bleak. "Fuck, Leona—I'm so sorry."

The reality of what we've done—it crashes down. Lands on me like the old chapel ceiling caving in.

His job.

My degree.

We've risked *everything.*

Oh God. What have we done?

Mason

The moment I saw Leona in that white robe at Graphite, a part of me knew it would end like this. I was already so far gone for her, already shamefully obsessed, and once I saw all of her...

This was inevitable.

That doesn't stop shame from clogging my throat when I see her wide-eyed shock. The tremble in her hands as she scrambles up, dressing quickly.

"We just—she saw—what are we—"

She's speaking in fragments. Too horrified to slow down. And I know how she feels, because seeing her upset, seeing what I've done to her...

I'm a monster.

"Leona." Her name is a plea. "I'll fix this. I'll make it right."

"How can you?" She's not even looking at me, fastening her jeans with clumsy fingers as she stares at the wall. "Your job—my degree—"

"You won't be punished." If there's one assurance I can give her, it's that. "I'll take full responsibility. This is my fault, Leona, and I won't let you suffer for my bad choices."

"Bad… choices…"

She sounds numb. Lost somewhere inside herself. I want to go to her and wrap her in my arms; I want to kiss her with every ounce of the longing still burning through me and tell her that she's mine.

But I've done enough damage. I won't make this worse. Not even when she finally looks over at me, tears swimming in her chocolate brown eyes, her arms hugging her waist.

"Go home." I take her by the elbow, allowing myself that one final touch. Her jacket is cool against my palm, so different from her soft, heated skin. She lets me lead her to the classroom doorway, her footsteps slow over the tiles. "Try to get some rest. When you come back to college tomorrow, this will already be over. You can finish your degree, work on your art, and you won't ever have to see me again."

"But…"

I wait for her to finish that sentence, my heart lodged somewhere in my throat. If she doesn't want that, if she even *hints* that she still wants me too—

Leona sighs, her shoulders slumping. "Okay."

My chest caves in. My ribs collapse, snapping and tangling, my heart a bloody lump inside the wreckage. But outwardly, I nod and force a smile.

"Good girl."

It's surreal, clearing up the mattress and easel. Putting away pieces of equipment that I've used a thousand times before in my classes, but that now feel like they should be sacred. Kept behind glass in a museum somewhere—a tribute to Leona.

To her first time with a man.

174

I truly am a monster.

* * *

Dean Gibson can always be relied upon to work late. It's gotten worse in the last few weeks, the light in his office shining for hours after campus has closed, and a few times I've debated asking him whether there's something he's avoiding at home.

I haven't, obviously. He's effectively my boss, and besides—neither of us is exactly chatty. But faint curiosity still needles at me as I approach his office, a strip of lamplight glowing beneath the door.

My knuckles rap against the wood.

There's a hearty sigh. And a deep voice calls: "Please, Charlotte. Have mercy."

I linger for a long moment—who the hell is Charlotte?—then roll my eyes and push the door open. I don't have time to play games. I need to fix this for Leona.

"Professor Reeve. Mason." The Dean straightens behind his desk, eyebrows twitching up in surprise. "I didn't realize anyone was still here."

I step inside and close the door behind me. Maybe we're the only two left on campus, but I'm done taking risks for tonight.

The Dean's office is just like the man himself: clean, classic and masculine. There's a large wooden desk, a waxy potted shrub beside the wall, and a white-faced clock ticking away the seconds. Bookshelves are crammed full—not with showy hardbacks that no one ever reads, but with textbooks, notepads, dog-eared treatises, and even a few spy novels.

I'm relieved to see a painting on the wall: an oil study of a lighthouse battered by storms. And a driftwood sculpture rests on his desk, acting as a paperweight.

Good. No man who appreciates art could be wholly awful.

"I've fucked up." No point beating around the bush. There's no sugarcoating what I've done. And I'm eager to get this over with, to get back out into the dark streets where my pounding heart feels more at home. "I slept with a student."

Dean Gibson blinks, his piercing eyes sharpening on me.

"Explain," he raps out. Already, a thousand plans for damage control and student care are rattling through that enormous brain.

"Leona Ridley. An art major. I... seduced her. In the classroom."

"In the—" the Dean breaks off, pinching the bridge of his nose. Yeah, I've really made a mess of this one.

"There's more."

His palm slams down on the desk. An angry flush is creeping over his cheeks above his trimmed dark beard. "*More?*"

"Yes." I grip my hands behind my back, squeezing so tight my knuckles creak. "Someone walked in on us. One of the art department staff."

How insidious is it that the memory makes my cock swell? I cough, mentally willing it down.

"For fuck's sake," Dean Gibson growls. "Have you lost your damn mind?"

It's a rhetorical question, clearly, but I answer it anyway.

"Yes." I shrug, outwardly casual even as a storm rages in my chest. "I'm in love with her. But I shouldn't have done it."

"No. No, you fucking shouldn't have." He leans back in his chair, scrubbing both hands over his face, mussing up his normally neat black hair. This is the end of my career, but I watch him dispassionately.

It doesn't matter.

Only Leona matters.

"Are we done?" I ask at last, when I'm tired of watching him curse under his breath. "Do you need anything else?"

He splutters. "Of course we're done. You're fired, Mason. Get the hell off my campus."

I nod. This is what I expected. What I came here for. But—

"What about Leona?" He stares at me, face wooden. I press on. "Will she be punished for this? I assure you, I am fully to blame."

"Get out," Dean Gibson snarls, and if I were a smaller man, I might flinch. "Of course she won't be punished. She's not the problem here, *you* are."

He says it with loathing, but a weight lifts off my shoulders. I stride out of his office twenty pounds lighter.

I fucked up. I know I did. And I'm ready to face the consequences. But if Leona had to suffer too…

I couldn't have lived with myself.

***

When the office buildings shut and the lamplights flick on, Graphite begins to stir. It may be an art studio, it may even offer day classes, but artists are nocturnal creatures. When other places are locking up their doors, Graphite is only just coming alive.

"Mason!" Fran is never less than delighted to see me. To see *anyone.* Her greeting is like a cup of warm tea. "I didn't expect you tonight."

"Neither did I." I hold up the canvas I sketched with Leona last time I was here. "Do you mind?"

Something settles over her face. Something knowing and amused. She waves an arm toward the back of the studio, her shawls shifting with the motion.

"Of course not. Help yourself."

I could tell her. Here, I could confess my sins, and even if Fran disapproved, she'd never toss me out. The words line up on my tongue, ready to spill out and damn me in her eyes, but I can't bring myself to say them.

Not because I care if she hates me. Not really. She's a good friend, but that is all.

But because what happened with Leona was the most precious moment of my life—regardless of the fallout.

I want to keep it secret a while longer. I want to hoard the memory of her like dragon treasure.

"She was good, wasn't she?"

My head jerks towards Fran. The gallery owner stands at my shoulder, peering at my canvas while I set up my easel. Tonight, I will begin to paint. To add texture and color and life.

"… Yes," I say when my pulse has calmed. Fran is talking about modeling. Nothing more.

"A natural muse."

If only they knew. All those paintings and sketches and portraits of Leona, locked up in that cupboard…

Somehow I doubt Dean Gibson will send them on.

"She is perfect." I turn and scowl at my sketch. I'll never *truly* capture Leona's beauty. The curl of her dark hair; the constellation of her freckles. "It's something of a torment."

"Tread carefully there." Her words are soft. Not judgmental, just... concerned.

I don't turn my head. "It's too late for that, Fran."

She squeezes my shoulder. And I blow out a long breath and pick up a brush.

Leona

When I get to campus early the next day, blinking in the morning sunshine, I march straight to Mason's office. There are a hundred things I wanted to say to him, starting with: *let's do that again.*

I don't care that we were caught. I don't care if people know. I don't want him to lose his career, obviously, but the way he talked… that didn't seem like his main worry anyway.

He was sorry. He thought he *hurt* me. I need to tell him that's not true. I should have told him last night, but I was too dazed with shock. Everything that happened—it was so overwhelming.

But when I knock on his office, the door swings open, and the room inside is empty.

Shelves without books.

A clean desk.

Even the storage cupboard hangs open, its shelves completely cleared.

I stand in the doorway, blood rushing in my ears, my limbs

turning rigid. The chatter grows louder behind me, the corridors filling with students, and still I stand there. Staring.

Finally, a throat clears behind me.

"Leona, I presume?"

My neck is stiff with tension as I turn. A man stands in the corridor, his jaw tense and the corners of his eyes creased with sympathy. It takes me a moment to recognize his neat black hair and his short beard, but when I do...

"Dean Gibson," I mumble. "Crap."

He blinks, taken aback, but I don't stick around to hear him yell at me. If they're going to leave a mark on my student record, so be it. I can't be here right now. Not when Mason is gone. I turn on my heel and plunge down the corridor. My boots slap against the tiles, my thighs burning in my jeans, then cool morning air nips my cheeks as I shove out of the art department doors and spill onto the stone path.

Where would he go? How can I find him?

I don't know where he lives. Don't even have his number.

There's no way for me to reach him.

For a crazy moment, I think about going to Charlotte and asking her to swipe his details from the system. But no—if he wanted me to know those things, he'd have told me them himself, right?

He's just gone.

Without a word of goodbye.

And he left me no way to reach him.

"Oh god." My lips are numb. I stagger across campus, my boots dragging on the path. Avery's still at home, and Paige spent the night at Raphael's. I'm... there's no one...

My feet turn towards the Dean's office anyway.

Not to see the man. To see his assistant. And not to steal an address, but to cry on her shoulder.

I've screwed this up so badly. And now I've lost the only man who's ever haunted my dreams.

* * *

"We have to think about this. You know, be strategic." Charlotte sits beside me an hour later, frowning out at the quad over the rim of her takeout latte. The second I turned up at her desk, nose red and eyes wet, she took my wrist and dragged me out to this bench.

At one point, Dean Gibson noticed us as he strode across the quad, and he changed direction for us. But Charlotte shook her head, giving him this *look*, and he rolled his eyes but walked away.

For a boss and his assistant…

Their relationship is weird.

"Where does he go? You know, other than here?"

I chew my bottom lip. Mason chatted with me a few times in class, but he never gave those kinds of details. Personal stuff. The only place I've ever seen him off campus is…

"Graphite. The art studio in the city."

I can't go there. It's too desperate, too tragic, and what if he turns me away? What if there's a reason he didn't say goodbye, and if I track him down, all I'll get is rejection?

"Forget it." Charlotte's mouth twists, but I nudge her with my shoulder. "If it's meant to be, it'll be. Let's talk about something else."

She hums, thinking for a second, then brightens. "I rescued

a kitten last week."

It's perfect. Exactly the kind of distraction I need: one with poofy brown fur and whiskers. Charlotte shows me tons of photos and videos, giggling down at the screen on her phone. And I shuffle closer, glad for her warmth and her company.

It's not all bad, I tell the hollow pit in my chest.

There are still kittens.

* * *

I stay away for a week. That's long enough to be normal, right? To be able to attend my free class at Graphite without seeming like a stalker? I wasn't sure if I should go at all, if I should write it off as a lost cause, but I want my free stained glass tuition, damn it.

Art is keeping me sane right now. I've thrown myself into it, heart and soul. And I thought I was obsessed before, thought I was fully immersed in the art world, but now there's a constant cramp in my hand and chalk under my fingernails, and the scent of turpentine follows me like a cloud.

Good to know I'll repel all other men too. Not that I care what any of them think.

The only person who might like my new perfume is long gone.

"One, please." I force a smile for the girl on reception at Graphite, handing over my voucher from Fran. The lobby is lit with a soft glow, hung stylishly with trailing plants, and god, I'm glad to be back.

This is what I need. More than anything, I need to forget

myself for a few hours. To quiet the endless frantic thoughts, spinning in circles around my mind, and find some blissful focus.

It doesn't hurt that there are stained glass windows in the old chapel. That even in this workshop, I can find a way to be closer to Mason. And for the next few hours, that's what I do: I sink deeper inside myself, and express myself through art.

I don't think.

I don't fret.

I barely remember to breathe.

And little by little, I start to feel better. So much better, that when I step back into the lobby with dry eyes and stiff shoulders, there's a genuine smile on my face.

"Leona?"

My heart slams in my chest. I stumble to a halt, but I don't turn.

It's probably not him. I'm probably projecting, making someone else's voice into his. Or worse—maybe I'm hallucinating. But then footsteps echo across the lobby, and a pair of broad shoulders come into view, wrapped in forest green sweater.

"Leona," he murmurs, and it's him. It is. I dare a glance, flicking my eyes up to his.

Professor Reeve stares down at me, his eyebrows drawn together and dark shadows under his eyes. He's not the calm, collected man who taught me for so long.

He looks exhausted.

"I'm sorry," I blurt, wincing as the words bounce around the lobby. I lower my voice and try again. "I'm so sorry about your job, professor."

He huffs a laugh. "Not a professor anymore."

Exactly. This is all my fault. If I hadn't pushed him, trying to be near him so often—

"Besides. I was tired of teaching anyway."

He's taking this so lightly. He looks *amused*, but there's sadness there too, tightening his green eyes. My hand twitches towards him, but I pull it back.

If he wanted my comfort, he would have said goodbye.

"Okay," I rasp. I'm suddenly so thirsty, with a headache brewing between my temples. "Well. Goodbye, Mason. Um. Good luck with everything."

"Leona, wait." His words stop me in my tracks. "I know I have no right to ask this, but please—don't go yet. Give me—give me a couple more minutes with you. Then I'll leave you alone, I swear."

Um. What?

His words are all wrong. That's not what's happening here. But when I look at him more closely, I see it now—the hollow to his cheeks. The desperate light in his eyes. The strength of his yearning, so powerful, my knees almost buckle.

Right. Oooh-kay then. I steel myself, then take his wrist.

"Professors are supposed to be clever," I whisper. "Why did you leave me if you still want me?"

"Leona…" He steps forward, then freezes. His features harden. "Come with me."

He leads me back up the Graphite stairwell, his wrist still clutched in my hand. Our footsteps echo, the only sound in the thick silence, but even though he doesn't speak, his body still tells me things.

Like his pulse, racing against my fingertip.

That tells me something.

That tells me a lot of things.

"In here."

It's a small studio. A private workspace—the kind that the professional artists rent for their big pieces. The big window is dark, only the pinpricks of stars shining through the glass, but Mason flicks on a table lamp. A warm glow fills the space, and I see it then: the easel in the center of the room.

There's a canvas, unfinished but already beautiful. A riot of bright colors and bold lines—a study in passion.

And the woman in the painting...

It's me.

"You should see the ones I drew of you before this ever happened." Mason strolls to my side, frowning at his work with a critical eye. "But I don't think the Dean will give me them back," he adds drily. "Probably for the best."

"I don't..." I clear my throat, mind racing. The ones he drew *before?* "I don't understand."

"Don't you?" Mason blows out a harsh breath, then turns to me, eyes glinting. "Then let me show you."

He's behind me before I know what's happening, his toned chest heaving against my back. I stare at his painting of me, with its lush tones and flowing lines, as he scrapes his teeth up the side of my neck.

"I've wanted you so long." He nips my earlobe, the pain sharp and fleeting. Warmth gathers in my core. His body heat is a wall at my back, his arm muscles rigid when he wraps me up, cages me in. "You have no fucking idea, my little muse. No idea how much you've consumed me."

He inhales deeply through his nose, breathing in the scent of my hair. And he crowds closer, his hard length jutting against the small of my back.

"Do you want this too?" His hips are already rocking against me. He can't help it. And I love that—I love how unraveled he's become. "Because if you don't, you need to say so quickly. Before I bury myself back home in your sweet cunt."

"I…" I can't find the words. And he *snarls*, sucking a bruise onto my skin. I fall back against him, my legs barely holding me up, the ache so fierce now that I can barely think straight.

"Yes," I pant at last. "I want it. I want *you*."

He doesn't waste another second. He marches me to the wall and wrenches my jeans down my hips. I only have time to brace my palms before he's there, notching at my entrance, driving deep inside me.

"*God.*"

I push back, rocking eagerly, already wet and ready since the moment I felt his pulse tapping against my fingertip. Mason fucks me hard and rhythmic, his palm cracking against my bare ass, and I tip back my head, my lips parting on a silent scream.

We cling together, desperate and vicious.

Yes.

I've missed him so much.

This is it. This is what we lost our minds over. This snarling, animal need. And it's more than just sex, more than two bodies coming together—it's our souls twining together in the darkness. I catch a glimpse of the easel out of the corner of my eye, and the reminder of his obsession—it makes me moan.

"Yes." His palm cracks against me harder, then he grips my hips and holds me in place, merciless. "You're mine, Leona. *Mine.* And I'm fucking yours. I'm going to bury myself in your sweet pussy every day for the rest of our lives."

I'm nodding, teeth chattering, and it's like hearing poetry. Like the world's most beautiful sonnet.

I don't care that it's rough. That his words are crude.

That's why I like it.

Mason reaches around, plunging his hand between my legs, and rubs at my clit, slow and teasing. The contrast of his smooth fingers against the brutal slam of his hips—it empties my lungs.

"I love you," he growls, and the way he says it—it's like a threat. "I love you, do you hear me?"

"Yes." My hands slip lower against the wall. "I l-love you too—"

He groans, pulling out of me, and spins me around. His hands hitch beneath my thighs, lifting me and crushing me against the wall, then he's back inside me and I can breathe again. He kisses me hard, pouring all his longing and lust and his possessiveness into the kiss.

I come with a squeak. It's muffled by his mouth, but he must feel the way my core clenches, the waves shuddering through me. Because he slams closer, deeper, and groans against my mouth as he spills inside me, filling me up.

It goes on for so long, pulse after pulse of his cock.

Honestly, it's almost funny.

"Jesus Christ," he mutters when he finally eases out. He sets me down on wobbly legs. "You're going to kill me. I'll be dead in a week."

"Dehydration?"

He throws a sharp look at me, then melts into a wry smile. "But what a way to go."

Mason

Five years later

I don't remember the last time I painted something other than my wife. Oh, I've done the odd commission. It's a terrible necessity, now that I'm working solely as a painter. But those works don't register on the same soul-deep level, and I forget them as soon as they're gone.

She's my muse. Even when I resolve to paint something or someone different this time, it's her face that peers out at me from the canvas. Those gorgeous eyes crinkled in amusement, as if to ask: *Who exactly do you think you're kidding?*

Leona's just as bad. That's my only defense. When she showed me her coursework for her senior college project, I nearly choked on my tongue.

Study after study of me. My face, my body. My arms wrapped around a waist which could only be hers. The students had an exhibition on campus, and her work was shown in pride of place, and according to my wife's friend

189

Charlotte, Dean Gibson nearly had a heart attack.

Now, we paint together. In a shared studio, our easels back to back. And while I paint her, Leona paints someone else: our son, sleeping quietly in his crib.

"He won't always be like this, you know." I keep my voice to a murmur, our studio calm except for the soft scrape of paintbrushes. "Soon he'll be crawling everywhere. Finger painting the walls. Spilling water all over the canvases."

"Grouch," Leona scolds, but she's smiling at her work. She knows full well how much I adore our child. And it's just as well, because her stomach is swollen behind the old shirt she likes to paint in. Another one of my shirts that she stole.

It's early days, but already I can't stop thinking about this new baby. Nor the healthy glow to Leona's cheeks.

She looks good pregnant.

Delicious.

I roll my head on my neck, forcing myself to concentrate. My brush swirls in the paint, sweeping up a glob of color, but no—it's no use. The brush clatters to my palette and I march around the easel.

"Come with me. Quickly."

She lets me tug her away, giggling. "The baby—"

"We'll stay close. Come on, little muse."

Once my blood heats near my wife, there's nothing else for it. I need to bury myself in her perfect heat; need to fuck the desperate longing away.

She doesn't mind. She grasps for me just as frantically, which is a relief, because this hunger will never fade. I know it as well as I know my own name.

She's my wife.

My salvation.

The center of my world.

"Take me," she breathes against my throat.

I plan to.

IV

The Dean

Description

You know what's worse than crushing on your boss?

When he's also your dad's best friend.

I moved across the country to get a fresh start. To see what I can make of myself away from my overbearing parents.

It was only supposed to be temporary—staying in Dean Gibson's spare room. I'd get a job, get my own place, and start my shiny new life.

But the Dean is so addicting. His calm presence makes my heart pound. And even though he's determined to keep his distance, he can't seem to let me go either.

Between his house and his office, we're barely apart. And he's cracking under the tension…

Charlotte

I stretch out on the sofa with a sigh, my new kitten balanced on my stomach. Truffle was a battered little scrap when I rescued her, an underfed ball of dull brown fur peering up at me with sad eyes from a cardboard box. But a whole week of proper kitten food and napping on my bed has brightened her blue eyes and rounded out her little belly.

"You're so beautiful, aren't you? Aren't you, Truffle?"

She purrs at me, her paws kneading at my stomach. I wince—her claws are like tiny needles—but I don't push her off.

We both need this cuddle.

I haven't been scooped out of a soggy cardboard box, but it feels like it lately. When I left home and flew across the country over a month ago, I couldn't stop beaming with excitement.

A new life! A blank slate! I had so many plans. I *still* have those plans, damn it. I want to start a photography business, move into my own place, and start living the life I've been daydreaming about for so long.

But... it's harder than I thought it would be. Taking those first steps on my own. Building a whole new life from scratch. I'd never admit it out loud to anyone, but sometimes...

I'm not sure I'm cut out for this.

Maybe my parents were right about me.

"*Such* a beautiful girl." Truffle's purr rattles in the silent living room as she marches in a circle, then flops down and curls into a ball. My fingertips trace her soft fur, the outline of her pointy ears, and the pink nub of her tiny nose.

This, at least, is one thing I've done right. Rescuing this fluffy bundle of love. And it's even a good business move, too—can't start a pet photography business without a portfolio.

Truffle's going to be my star. The money-maker.

She's plenty cute enough. Cute as pie.

Ten sharp claws dig into my stomach, needling my bare skin through my tank top. I hiss, wincing as I peel her paws away.

Kind of cute, anyway.

The scrape of a key in the front door stiffens my spine. I stay stretched out, feigning casualness, even as my ears strain for the first steps on the floorboards.

Step.

Step.

Behind me, I feel him pause in the doorway.

He always does this—checks in on me. It's the first thing he does when he finally gets home. And that time gets later and later each day, until the sky is tinged navy through the windows and I've almost given up on waiting for him each night.

Almost.

I'd wait an embarrassingly long time for this man.

"You're late." My voice is light. Casual. It betrays no hint

197

of the knot in my stomach; the tension that sparks and flares under my skin whenever he's near.

James Gibson.

The college Dean.

And my father's best friend.

"You should keep me late, too." Finally, I turn my head, resting my cheek on the sofa cushions. James watches me closely, one shoulder leaning on the door frame, his hands deep in his pockets. His dark hair and beard are striking against his pale skin, and his shirt clings to his broad chest. "I'm your assistant, after all. I could *assist*."

A tired smile tugs his mouth.

"That's hardly fair." His rich baritone makes me shiver, my body shifting restlessly on the sofa. "You have far better things to do than work overtime with me."

Wrong.

I mean, sure—admin is pretty dull. I'm not obsessed with photocopying or anything. But it's so much worse leaving the Dean's office with him in it, and traipsing home to this silent house where every room reminds me of him.

The sturdy bookshelves, crammed to overflowing with books.

The surprisingly sensual sculptures, acting as paperweights.

Hell—even the comfy gray sofa, with its soft throw and big screen TV. The first night I arrived here, we watched a movie together, trying to get to know each other for the first time in five years. I hadn't seen James since I was sixteen, but I remembered his kind eyes and his rumbling laugh from my childhood.

Still, it was... awkward. Something between us was different. His eyes heated when they landed on me, his eyebrows twitching in shock, and my body tingled in response.

We haven't watched a movie together since. It's been kind of lonely.

Especially when he keeps working later and later. Almost like... he's avoiding me.

"I found two more apartments." I force the words out, even as a big part of me resents them. I *know* I can't stay here much longer, can't overstay my welcome, but it's so hard to look for other places when James' steady presence is *here.* Yes, he's familiar and safe, a man I've known for years, but it's more than that. James makes me feel settled.

Truffle likes it here too. She's allowed on the sofa. And she plays with the handle of James' gym bag.

But I won't be selfish, won't cause more trouble than I already have, so I push on. "Shall I book us some viewings?"

When I started looking for apartments in my first week, James insisted on coming to view them with me. To make sure I don't get ripped off, or to keep me safe from strangers—who knows? Either way, I liked it. It made warmth bloom in my chest. Just like when he came home two days in, telling me to get an early night because he'd found me a job in his office.

It's nice to have someone looking out for me.

James works his jaw, frowning down at the rug for a long moment, then says: "Send me the links first."

Ooo-kay. They're studio apartments, not drug dens, but he can vet them first if he likes. All it will do is slow the process down, and I'm on board with anything that keeps me here longer.

Here, where I can hear his steady breathing. Where his clean, masculine scent clings to the furniture. Where I can hear the drumming of the shower spray through my bedroom wall and know that he's close, that he's naked, drops of heated water trickling over the sculpted muscles of his chest, and *god*—

I really need to move out. I'm turning into such a pervert.

"Are you busy tonight?"

I blink at his question. Usually, he ducks his head in on me, makes sure I'm still alive, then disappears into his study. Sometimes he'll fix a quick dinner in the kitchen; sometimes he's already eaten. Either way, I don't feature in his plans.

"Um." I glance down at the sleeping kitten. Her belly rises and falls with each puffed breath. "No?"

James nods, the movement sharp, then grinds out another question. Forces the words between his teeth, like they cost him. "Would you like to watch a movie?" I stare at him, bemused, and he gusts out a sigh. "I've been neglecting you."

No. That's not true. I'm a grown woman, not a child—I don't need constant entertainment. Have I been lonely, rattling around this house on my own in the evenings? Sure. Have I made it worse by pining for this man like a war widow? Definitely.

But James hasn't done anything wrong. He's got way better things to do than hang around with someone half his age.

"It's fine," I rasp, my throat weirdly tight. Why do I crumble at the slightest sign of care? "You're busy. And you didn't ask for me to gatecrash your house."

My father did that. It was something about wanting me to stay with someone trustworthy. Just until I found my feet.

But James' head twitches, his mouth flattening in a line, and when he speaks again, it's an order.

"We're going to spend some time together, Charlotte."

A slow smile spreads over my face.

Finally.

* * *

When I was a little kid, my parents used to host these big parties. Fancy dinners and drinks for wealthy businessmen—rich investors and powerful politicians. All the strangers in the house used to keep me awake, too freaked out to sleep in my pink princess bed. So they'd set me up in my father's study, on a sofa one of the staff dragged in there specially. And I'd watch hours and hours of kids' movies—an endless loop of handsome princes and cartoon animals.

No one knew I was in there. My parents were ambitious, but not stupid. They'd never risk my safety, and to be doubly sure, they set a trusted staff member to watch outside the study door until all the strange men were gone. The only person they let through was my father's best friend.

James.

They knew and I knew—hell, the whole world knew—that James was the most honorable man on the continent. He'd rather chop off a limb than scare a little girl. So when James poked his head around my father's study door, checking in on me at the parties, my face used to light up.

"James! Come and watch with me!"

He always did, too. Not for long—the party was waiting—but long enough to calm me down and make me feel cared for. He asked about the movies; which characters were my favorite; what I thought might happen next. He'd sit at the other end of the sofa, tugging at his too-tight shirt collar, the TV screen washing him blue. Exhaustion lined his handsome face—he was never keen on those parties. And when he ruffled my hair and disappeared back through the doorway, I'd stare at the space where he'd just been like I could magic him back.

That was years ago. Back when I was a child and he was a grown man; back when things were simpler. Clean cut between us.

I'm not a child anymore. I'm twenty one years old.

But I wouldn't mind if he ruffled my hair.

"It's just like old times." I rest my chin on me knees as James strides into the living room carrying a tray. It's set with a bowl of warm popcorn, the scent making my stomach growl, and two steaming mugs of hot chocolate.

James flicks me a wry look. "Not quite. Some things are very different."

He means me. His eyes rake over me as he sets the tray on the coffee table, darting and guilty, almost like he can't help himself. And my limbs heat where I'm curled on the sofa, Truffle sleeping on the arm beside me.

I wrap my arms tighter. "You're still looking out for me. Taking care of me, even though I'm not your problem."

James turns to sit at the other end of the sofa, but not before I see a shadow pass behind his eyes. I wait, but all he says is: "What would you like to watch?"

We settle on an action movie. It feels safest, somehow. And as the opening credits fade into the first car chase, I slump against the cushions and let out a sigh.

What is it about sitting in the half-dark with someone that feels so freaking intimate? Curled up just a few feet away from James, I swear I can hear every soft breath. Every rustle of his shifting body against the sofa. And it's not just my hearing that's going beserk—my other senses are suddenly heightened too. The colors on the TV screen are so vivid I have to look away; the rasp of the sofa fabric against my bare legs makes my nerves spark and my teeth clench. I shove handful after handful of popcorn in my mouth, so nervous that I need to keep moving.

"You're hungry," James says softly after half the bowl's gone. "I should have brought you dinner."

My cheeks flush. Well, this is embarrassing.

"No, um. It's okay. I already ate." Plus, I can feed myself. I'm not *that* incapable.

James smiles at me, his eyes crinkling at the corners, and for a minute, I forget to look at the screen. I'm too wrapped up in the blue light flickering over his cheekbones, his throat, the shadowed dip of his collarbone visible beneath his open shirt. Then he swallows, turning back to the movie, and the moment is gone.

"You've been working late a lot." I wait until a quiet scene to ask the question that's been gnawing my insides. "Are you tired of having me here?"

James' head jerks towards me, his eyes flaring. "No," he grinds out. "I'm never tired of you."

"Because those apartments looked totally fine. I could go and see one tomorrow—"

"Charlotte." He says my name like an order. And god help me, shivers race over my skin, my nipples tightening under my tank top. James turns to me fully, fixing me with his stern gaze. "Listen to me: I do not want you gone."

I'm nodding. Bobbing my head like an idiot, too dazed to say anything else. And James watches me closely for a minute, until he's satisfied that I've listened. Then he nods once, and turns back to the screen.

Back to explosions and gun fights, and none of it half as chaotic as my insides.

I duck my head and stroke Truffle, hiding my smile.

* * *

"Dean Gibson? Really?" My new friend Paige leans closer across our table, her giant sweater shifting on her narrow shoulders. We're in the campus coffee shop with her two roommates, Avery and Leona, clutching hot mugs of coffee and catching up on my lunch break. Paige isn't usually here, too busy rehearsing ballet, so she's never heard about my shameless crush before.

"What's wrong with him?" I sit up straighter, defensive. These girls are amazing, the best friends I've made here, but I can't stand to hear bad words about James.

"Nothing," Paige says quickly, holding up two delicate hands. "He's just so… so *strict*."

"Yeah," I hum, relaxing again. Leona snorts at my dreamy smile. "He is."

Avery's already giggling, the motion shaking the table and her blonde braids, but I don't care. If there's one thing I'm not embarrassed about, it's my taste in James Gibson. He's the perfect man, so handsome and calm, so quietly assertive. I've made plenty of dumb decisions, but liking him? That's not one of them.

Letting myself slowly fall for him, on the other hand…

Yeah, that's pretty dumb. I really need to move out.

"Isn't he your boss?" Leona asks.

I point at her. "Pot, kettle, black. What about Mason?"

"Professor isn't the same as boss—"

"Sure it is."

We bicker gamely, snarking at each other over our mugs, but when my break is up, I sweep them each into a tight hug in the quad. "Come here," I mumble into Leona's dark wavy

204

hair. "Don't hold out. Let your older-man-seduction-powers rub off on me."

"Ew." She pulls away, laughing. "Get your own."

"Believe me," I tell her drily. "I'm trying."

I'm not, though. I may joke with the girls, but the truth is, whenever James is near, I freeze. The thought of telling him how I feel, of *flirting*, even—my throat closes up.

Because what if I lose him? What if I piss him off so badly, he never wants to see me again? What if he tells my dad?

Worst of all, what if James finds my crush disgusting?

I can't risk it.

So I'll keep smiling at him, and asking casual questions about his day, and teasing him when we're alone in the office. I'll keep finding excuses to knock on his door, to spend time together, to be in the warm glow of his presence.

And it will be enough.

It will.

It has to be.

James

When I agreed to host Parker Young's little girl for a few months, in my head, she was still sixteen. A sweet girl, funny and smart, but a *girl*. Someone to look out for and keep company, but no one that would turn my world on its head.

More fool me. Because funnily enough, Charlotte is not sixteen anymore. Time did not stand still since the last time I saw her. She's a young woman now, all hints of adolescence gone, and from the moment I picked her up at the airport, I've been cursing my poor judgment.

The way she looks at me with those wide, pale eyes… She's triggered something inside me. Dark, primal urges—to touch, to protect, to *claim*. To stamp myself all over her as surely as she's written on me, and to never let her out of my grip again.

What would Parker say if he knew the way my heartbeat races around his daughter? If he knew how my hands ache to touch her waist, how my fingers long to twine through her glossy blonde hair?

She's been here just over a month, and already I've jacked

off more times than I can count. Just catching whiffs of her feminine scent around my house, seeing her gorgeous hourglass figure bend over her desk at the office—

It's torture. I need her gone.

And yet, I got her a job in my office, ensuring I'd see her every weekday. And *yet*, every time Charlotte finds a potential apartment, I pick holes in it. Find excuses to keep her here with me.

I know she'll go eventually. Hell, I'll help her move; I'll install a security lock on her door. But even though it makes me the worst kind of man, I can't help but drag this out as long as possible.

Because once she's gone, once my house is cold and empty, devoid of her scent again... My life will be black and white once more. Without color.

"Charlotte." I press the button on my office phone which puts me through to her. It's dangerous, having a direct line to her this way. I have to stop myself from eavesdropping on her calls, listening to her sweet voice. "Come here for a moment, please."

Through the wall, I hear the scrape of her chair. Her light footsteps, muffled by the rug. The Dean's office has an old-fashioned layout—my office in the center, then my assistant's in an antechamber outside. All it means is that Charlotte is constantly in the most maddening place possible—out of sight, but within earshot. On my mind, but not within reach.

How am I supposed to get any work done when I can hear her sighing with boredom? When I can hear her fingertips tapping against the keyboard, and picture them drumming down the rigid muscles of my back instead?

A brief knock interrupts my thoughts, then the door swings

open.

"Yes?" She smiles at me brightly, always so pleased to be summoned. So naturally *giving*. I shift my chair further under the desk to hide the swelling in my pants.

"There's only an hour left. I have no other tasks for you today. You might as well take an early finish." Her face falls. I talk quickly, wanting to reassure her. To bring that bright smile back. "You'll still be paid for the full day, of course."

But her mouth stays turned down. "What about you?"

I clear my throat. There's no way I can tell her the truth. That I need a few hours without her here so I can think straight and get some damn work done.

"I'll be home late. Go ahead and eat without me."

Her face crumples.

Fuck.

I stand quickly, alarmed, my arousal forgotten as fast as it came. Charlotte wraps her arms around her waist, hugging herself, struggling to rein in her emotions. She's dressed in a white blouse and a pencil skirt, the fabric of her blouse sliding under her arms., and behind her, through the open doorway, the distant hum of conversation drifts down the corridor.

"Charlotte? What is it?"

She shakes her head. Forces a smile—but not the genuine one I want. It's superficial. Pained.

"Nothing." She hiccups a laugh, and it sounds bleak. "Don't worry. It's pathetic."

"What is?" I round the desk in three strides, crossing straight to her. The moisture brimming in her eyes cuts through my usual caution, and I take her by the elbows. Rub the pads of my thumbs over her arms. "Charlotte. Tell me what's wrong."

We're standing in the open doorway. Anyone walking past

could see this—the college Dean standing too close to his assistant, his hands on her bare skin. It's inappropriate, more wrong than anyone here could possibly know, and yet I can't step back. Can't put distance between us.

"Crap, this is embarrassing." Charlotte sniffles, staring at the center of my chest. Then, quietly, she admits: "I miss you."

God. *God.* I've been so wrapped up in ensuring I don't cross any lines, so determined to keep my attraction to her a secret, that I've let her feel neglected. Let her be lonely, like she was as a child.

Fuck. My breath saws in and out of my chest. The sounds of the corridor are muffled, like they're coming from far away.

"Forgive me." The words are choppy, but she rolls her eyes. Peeks up at me with a small smile.

"Don't be silly. There's nothing to forgive."

I squeeze her elbows. *"Forgive me."*

Her eyelids flutter closed, her sooty lashes casting shadows over her cheeks. "Okay," she breathes, so quiet I almost miss it. Then: "I'll see you tonight." She gathers herself, pushing her shoulders back.

"No." She jerks at my sudden harsh tone. "Change of plan. I need you here."

They're the words no assistant has ever wanted from their boss, but a flush spreads over Charlotte's cheeks. She's glowing. And ten minutes later, when I carry a chair in for her and set it at the end of my desk, she practically bounces over and flings herself into the seat.

"What are we working on?"

"Research funding," I mutter. It's always goddamn funding.

"Sounds boring."

I snort as I hand her a stack of forms to look through. "It is."

If I thought she was distracting through the wall, it's nothing compared to having her in the corner of my eye. Especially when she starts swinging her foot, the toe of her ballet flat brushing my leg.

I risk a glance. She frowns down at the forms, absorbed.

Not touching me on purpose, then. It's nothing. Nothing.

And of course it's fucking nothing, because she's a gorgeous young woman and I'm a cranky bastard twice her age. I clear my throat, roll my neck, and force myself to focus on the damn forms.

This is a job for her. I'm a boss; a family friend.

That's all.

* * *

Three days later, I walk into my living room after dinner and find Charlotte stretched out on the rug with a camera. The little brown kitten she rescued is posed on a stack of books by the fireplace, a nearby lamp casting the scene in a warm glow.

"What on earth are you doing?"

She twists a dial on her camera, eye glued to the lens. "Pet photography portfolio."

Right. Naturally.

"Did Truffle sign a release?"

She rolls her eyes, mouth twitching. "That's such a dad joke."

Silence thickens between us. The reminder of her father—of the gap in our ages—it crowds the room. I cough, suddenly awkward.

But then Charlotte rolls onto her back and props herself up by the elbows, and all other thoughts drain from my head.

She's in my shirt. A soft, faded white cotton t-shirt that

clings to her curves and pools on the rug beside her. It's far too big for her, the neckline draping over one shoulder, and my mouth is dry. I need water. No, screw that—I need something much stronger.

"It's for my business. For the social media channels." She chatters away, telling me about her plans, and I *am* listening, damn it, I want to hear all this, but I also can't keep my eyes off that shirt. "Oh, sorry." She plucks at the hem. "I felt like wearing something comfy so I stole it from the laundry. I hope you don't mind."

Mind? Do I *mind* her wearing my clothes? Getting her warmth, her sweet cherry scent on the fabric? Letting it slip off her shoulder and show a glimpse of her collarbone, a stray lock of her hair dangling down from her messy bun?

My teeth ache, my jaw is clenched so hard. I shake my head. "I don't mind."

"Oh, good." She smiles, relieved, and keeps talking, and I drag my gaze back up to her face. Even when her hips rock from side to side the tiniest fraction. Even when the hem slips and shows a sliver of bare stomach. She's squirming on the rug, restless, her cheeks flushed though she doesn't even seem to realize it. The way her body reacts to me standing above her.

I tear myself away and stride to the sofa. Sit safely away from her, where I can't get any ideas.

"What do you think of the lighting?" she asks, and we're back to normal. On safe topics. I breathe in hard through my nose, and answer.

* * *

211

Hours later, when stars shine through the kitchen window, I stand at the counter, washing up the dishes from dinner. The room is half-lit, the gloom making my fatigue worse, and I scrub at the plates with drowsy motions.

Click.

I glance over my shoulder, bleary. Charlotte leans in the doorway, her camera pressed to her eye. As I watch, she twists the lens, then presses the button.

Click.

"More for the portfolio?" My voice is quiet. As the evening wore on, a velvet hush settled over the house.

Charlotte shrugs one shoulder. "No. These are for me."

My heart thumps faster, even as I talk myself down. *She means nothing by that. She's being friendly. Polite.*

"You were better off with Truffle."

Her laugh is so quiet. A rush of breath. "I disagree." She cocks her head. "You make a very striking model."

Is that a good thing? Hell if I know. So I don't rush to do anything, drying up my hands with methodical swipes of the towel. When I finally turn and lean back against the sink, Charlotte raises her camera again.

Click.

"This is hardly fair." Her bare toes are scrunched against the tiles. I make a mental note to bring her home some warm socks. When I look back up, her lips are parted. "I don't have any of you."

She takes a halting step forward.

"You could. If you like." She holds out her camera, the expensive equipment hovering between us. I eye it doubtfully—all those settings and dials. I don't want to mess up her business.

"I don't think—"

She draws the camera back. "No. I guess not."

"Wait." I dig my phone out of my pocket, ignoring the voices screaming in my head to *stop*. That this is dangerous territory. "Here. Smile for me, Charlotte."

She doesn't smile. She places her camera carefully on the counter, then backs up to lean against the wall. Moonlight filters in through the window, ghostly pale against her stolen shirt, the hem dangling only a few inches above the bottom of her shorts. Her long legs cross at the ankles, her toenails painted ruby red, and I raise my phone.

"Perfect," I rasp, snapping a photo. "Now we're even."

It's bullshit, of course. She took some practice shots with her camera—shots that she's sure to delete the next time she sorts through them. Whereas I stole a photo that I'll never fucking delete. That I'll look at every day for the rest of my life. We're hardly even.

But that doesn't stop me from taking another. She lifts an arm, sweeping her hair back with one hand, and I take another. Another. I'm a man possessed, bewitched by what we're doing—by the way she's looking at me, filled with yearning. Charlotte poses for me like it's the most natural thing in the world, like she's read my mind and knows exactly how I'd like to see her.

Her hip cocked.

White teeth digging into her lip.

Stepping closer, her fingers playing at the hem of her t-shirt.

"Don't," I grind out as she begins to raise the fabric. She drops the shirt, her cheeks flaming in embarrassment. "Charlotte," I begin, but she's already turned on her heel, scurrying out of the kitchen.

I let out a groan, falling back against the sink. I did the right thing, stopping her. Didn't I?

There's no way she could know her effect on me. What she'd be tempting by pulling off that shirt.

She got swept up in the moment, the same as I did.

And I saved her from myself.

Charlotte

"It's not that bad."

I glare over the rim of my takeout coffee cup. "I nearly *flashed* him, Avery."

The English student bites her lip, visibly searching for something comforting to say. "At least he stopped you?" she offers weakly. She's bundled up in a soft pink scarf, the tips of her ears flushed where they meet the wind. I burrow deeper into my pea coat, wishing for the hundredth time that I packed better for the weather here.

It's not comforting that he stopped me. That's the *problem.* I wanted to undress for James; I *wanted* him to see all of me. To look at the pale expanse of my bare skin with the raw hunger I sometimes glimpse in his eyes.

Instead, I made a fool of myself. Threw myself at my father's best friend. I wasn't even thinking straight, I had no grand seduction plans. Just got swept up in the moment.

Oh god, what if he tells my dad?

"I need to move again." I slump down on the bench. "I can't

215

stay here. Not with James." Even as the words leave my mouth, sorrow fills me. Wrenches my heart. Because to him, I may be an annoying lodger. A hare-brained assistant who tried to cross a line. But to me...

He's become special. My anchor in rough waters.

Plus, I really hate moving. Packing is such a drag.

"That's a bit dramatic." Avery sucks hard on her straw, cubes of ice bobbing in her iced coffee. It's early fall, with a bite to the breeze and crisp golden leaves underfoot. We're huddled together on a bench against the chill, but she's still drinking iced lattes. Maniac. I sip my own cappuccino, humming as it warms my tongue.

"Is it? What would you have done if you'd flashed Ellis and he turned you down?"

She chews her lip, thinking, then gusts out a breath. "Probably faked my own death. But that doesn't make it a good idea, Charlotte! And besides—you didn't *actually* flash him."

"Because he was too horrified to let me."

She grunts, gnawing her straw. "That is pretty awkward."

"*Thank* you." It's not an argument that I'm thrilled to win. I knock my ankle boots together, scowling down at the scuffed leather. "Maybe I should go back home and stay with my parents like they wanted me to. Just while I set up my business."

"No." Avery's command snaps through the air. I turn to her, eyebrows raised. Avery's sweet; a blushing romantic—she's not exactly the bossy type. But she gathers herself up to her full seated height, pinning me with a glare. "You're not going back. You've come all this way, and you *can* do this. You can."

"But—"

"Your parents don't support your business idea, right?" I shake my head mutely. Pet photography is too cutesy for my parents; too gimmicky and embarrassing. I really need to stop going out for cocktails with the girls and blurting everything out. "Well, it's going to be hard enough anyway to go after your dream. Why do it surrounded by people who are hoping you'll fail?"

She's right. God. I sigh and shuffle closer, leaning my head on her shoulder. I'm a few inches taller, so I have to stoop like a weirdo, but it's worth it.

I've never had friends like this before.

"I can never look him in the eye again."

"Who, the Dean?"

I snort. "No, the guy who made our coffees."

"Don't look at him, then." She tucks her hand in the crook of my arm. "Avoid him until you find your own place. Then give him a thank you card and move on."

"Yeah." I stare at a patch of scraggly grass. It shouldn't hurt this much, thinking about going. Especially when I feel so awkward at home, I can barely sit still. I've set Truffle so on edge, she's been off her kitty biscuits. "I'll call about viewing some places this afternoon."

"Atta girl." Avery nudges me. "Maybe you can find somewhere close to us."

That would be nice. A small win after what sometimes feels like a lifelong parade of failures.

"I could come over for movie nights."

She clicks her tongue. "You can do that anyway. You know you're always welcome."

"Can you guarantee I won't see you sucking face with your professor?"

Avery smiles sweetly. "No promises."

* * *

His office door is closed again when I return to my desk. Guess I'm not the only one hiding from the awkwardness—I've barely caught a glimpse of James all day. I scowl at the thick wood as I unwind my scarf from my neck, dropping it into my in-tray.

Must he avoid me like this? It makes it all so much worse. Like he thinks I'm some crazed pervert who could lunge for him at any time.

No need to hide out, Dean Gibson. I got the message, loud and clear.

A muffled sob floats through the door and I stiffen, straining to hear. There's James' low, calming murmur, and someone else speaking too—a young woman, hiccuping through her sentences.

Poor thing. She's having a worse day than any of us. I shrug off my pea coat, hanging it on the peg on the wall, then gather up my Upset Student Supplies. Over the last few weeks, James and I have fallen into a good routine: he deals with the official stuff, takes the hard line in his office, and then I do the comforting bit afterward. I've starting keeping a box of tissues and a stash of chocolate bars in my desk just for times like this.

The door swings open, the sniffles coming louder, then a red-faced student is walked to my desk. James stands at her shoulder, jaw tense, but not because he's afraid of women crying.

Just of them flashing him in his kitchen.

"Charlotte. This is Danielle. Perhaps you could, ah..." He gestures at my spread of chocolates and tissues, already laid out. I've drawn up a second chair for her, ready and waiting.

Danielle—windswept black hair and a freckled nose behind glasses—drops into the seat, tugging two tissues out of the box. She screws up her eyes as she blows her nose, shaking her head from side to side.

"You've got it from here?" James murmurs, his steady eyes finding mine.

I nod, too tied up in knots to speak. And when he pats Danielle's trembling shoulder, a wave of irrational jealousy tears through me, so strong it steals my breath.

I want his hands on *me*. Me, and only me, damn it.

I grit my teeth and tamp those feelings down. No need to add 'crazy' to the list of my worst traits. James is being polite, utterly professional, and besides—it's not like I have a claim. I have no right to growl and snap over him like a she-wolf.

Even if I do want to drag him into his office and muss up his neat dark hair; want to suck my bruises all over his throat below his beard.

"Are you alright?" James peers down at me, concerned. I give myself a shake, then focus on Danielle.

"Fine. I've got this." He lingers for half a moment, then turns and retreats to his office.

He leaves the door open this time. Just a crack. But I stare at that six inches of space until my eyes go dry.

* * *

The crash echoes through the silent house. I sit bolt upright in bed, heart hammering, sweat beading my top lip. It takes a second for my brain to catch up, to realize what's happening.

It's late. The middle of the night. And I was sleeping, curled up alone in my guest bed, trying not to dream endlessly of

James Gibson's big hands tracing over my skin.

I strain to listen. There's no sound in the house—no creak of footsteps or murmur of voices. All I can hear is the *drip, drip* of the rain on the windowsill.

Crap. I've never dealt with anything like this before. We had a break in once when I was a little girl, but the alarm went off before the intruders even reached my floor. Still, I remember the raw fear of that night. The chilling realization that some people don't care about boundaries, or about you feeling safe. They'll invade your space; they'll shatter your peace without a second thought.

"Shit." My whisper is loud in the dark room. I shuffle to the edge of my bed, throwing the covers off. "Shit, shit, shit."

The floorboards creak as I swing my legs out of bed. I push to stand, a throw wrapped around my shoulders. My pajama shorts are tiny, barely more than hot pants, and James' white cotton t-shirt isn't exactly warm.

"Shit." I stare at my bedroom door, willing my feet to move. But my muscles are locked, rigid with tension, and my heart is racing so fast I feel lightheaded.

Come on, Charlotte Young. Are you a woman or a mouse?

A mouse. Definitely a mouse. But my feet shuffle forwards, dragging over the rug. Whoever has broken in had better not be here to fight, because I'm moving like a hundred year old woman.

"Ah!" I jump half a foot into the air the second I push my door open. There's a shape in the hallway, a man's shadow, and oh my god, this is how I die.

"Charlotte! Charlotte. It's me, sweetheart." Warm hands grip my shoulders, dragging me back to reality. James stands in front of me, his eyes shining in a shaft of moonlight. He's wearing dark green sweatpants and a fitted black t-shirt.

Okay. Is this a sex dream?

"You heard the crash?" he murmurs, thumbs rubbing at my collarbone.

Nope. Definitely awake. Got it.

"What do we do?" My whisper comes out strangled. I don't sound like someone starting a fancy new adult life; I sound like a scared teenager. But James' hands on me are warm and steady, my breaths slowing just from having him near.

"You're going to go back inside your room and lock the door." His deep voice is assured. *Dangerous.* "I'll take care of it."

But… what if there are weapons? Rabid dogs? Serial killers? "I—"

"Quickly, Charlotte." His tone brooks no argument. James crowds me back into my bedroom, his broad shoulders blocking any chance of escape, and like a wimp I let him do it. "Stay quiet. If I don't come and knock in fifteen minutes, call 911." He hovers for a second, the sharp planes of his face cast in shadow, then ducks down and kisses my forehead. The brush of his lips is so swift, by the time he turns away, I'm already convinced I dreamed it.

Oh, hell. I sway on the spot, squeezing the throw blanket in my fists, so freaking overwhelming by the last few minutes that my circuits are fried. It takes the creak of James' footsteps on the stairs to jerk me back to life, and then I'm moving. Striding on suddenly functional legs.

I'll wait up here, sure, but not in this cold, unfeeling guest room. This empty box, devoid of life or comfort. If I'm going to wait around like a sitting duck, I'm going to do it in the safest place I know.

Teacher's Pet

I slip through the hallway shadows and into James' bedroom.

James

The stairs creak as I descend the steps, holding my breath so I can strain to listen. There are no voices or thuds—no sign of another person. If the crash hadn't woken me, I'd never have thought there was someone here.

But that crash was unmistakable. It splintered the quiet, and wrenched us both awake.

There is someone in this house.

My blood thrums in my veins as I reach the hallway, turning the corner on silent steps. Every sense is heightened, dialed up to one hundred by the adrenaline—my quick eyes pick out layers of shadow; my tensed muscles are primed to fight.

I'm a rational man. If I were here alone, I'd think this through. I'd weigh up the pros and cons of investigating the noise myself, never mind the gut impulse to charge down the stairs and reclaim my home.

But Charlotte is here. And I can't be rational. I can't be careful and calm when someone is threatening her, when someone dares to come into my home and fill her with fear.

Whoever is in my house had better *hope* they're armed. I'm out for blood.

My bare feet are silent on the hallway rug. I keep close to the wall, where the floorboards are less likely to creak. For the dozenth time I wonder if we imagined it—if we were jerked awake by some shared hallucination. But then another crash shatters the quiet, a cacophony of china breaking against tiles.

I lunge into the kitchen, arms raised, ready to rain down fury on the intruder.

Truffle blinks at me from the kitchen floor.

The kitten is bedraggled and wide-eyed, her tiny body trembling as she huddles in a sea of shattered dishes. The drying rack is upside down against a cupboard; shards of white china litter the dark tiles like ice bergs.

"For fuck's sake." I scrub a hand down my face, feeling my racing heartbeat slow. There are no intruders. Just this wrecking ball of a kitten. Picking my way through the shards, I scoop her up by the scruff and hold her against my chest.

She's terrified. Her little heart is pounding so hard I can feel it through my t-shirt, and fuck, I can't punish a frightened animal. So for the next ten minutes, I cradle her to my chest, rubbing her gently with my thumb while I sweep up the china with the other hand. My eyes adjust to the shadows, helped by the moonlight, and it's not long before the wreckage is cleared.

I'll need to go over it again tomorrow, but it's safe enough for now. Charlotte won't slice her foot when she comes down for breakfast; that's the important thing.

"Little hellion," I murmur to the ball of quivering fur. She's calming slowly, her breaths steadying. "You're just like your owner. Did you know that? Bursting into my life and shattering my peace."

The stairs groan as I climb back upstairs. No need to tiptoe anymore. And though I'm calming too, settled by the relief of finding Truffle, my heart still stops when I see Charlotte's bedroom door.

It's open.

Not just unlocked, but *open.* How is this—where did she—

Something rustles in my bedroom. I swallow hard, staring at my own room, my heart picking up to a steady thud. Not from fear or adrenaline this time, but because she's *there.* In my space. Maybe even on my bed.

Fuck. I slam my eyes shut. Give myself a stern talking to, a reminder that she's a frightened young woman, that she wants nothing more from me than comfort. That I'm twice her age and have none of her vibrancy—I'm not a walking miracle the way Charlotte is.

"Keep it together," I mutter to the kitten. "You got us into this mess."

The door swings open under my palm. And Charlotte blinks at me, her knees tucked under her chin where she sits in the center of my bed. She's on top of the covers, still in that goddamn borrowed shirt, and her hair tumbles down her back in a glossy blonde tangle. The light from my bedside lamp casts her in a warm glow, but it doesn't hide the chalky white pallor of her face.

"James," she whispers. "You're okay. Oh my god." Her arms tighten around her knees, wrapping herself in a hug.

She was that worried about me? Fierce approval roars in my chest, never mind the knock to my ego.

"Here's our criminal." I drop Truffle on the covers by her bare feet. The kitten lurches straight for Charlotte, making a beeline for comfort. And I should *not* be jealous of a tiny animal, not even when Charlotte scoops her up and peppers kisses through her fur.

"Poor baby! What happened to you?"

"I believe Truffle happened to the kitchen."

Guilt and horror crowd Charlotte's face, and I wish I hadn't said anything. It doesn't *matter.* They're just dishes; they're not worth worrying over.

"Crap. I'm so sorry. I'll pay for the damage, I swear. You can take it out of my wages—"

I raise a palm and she falls quiet. "It's fine, Charlotte." She opens her mouth to argue, but I speak over her. "It's already forgotten."

She deflates, still so clearly on edge, and I hate this. Hate seeing her vulnerable and sad, curled up in the expanse of my bed.

That's why I do it. At least, that's the excuse I give myself. Why I pause for a moment, watching her, then round the bed and climb on behind her. I shuffle up to lean against the headboard, still firmly above the covers, and hold up one arm.

"Come here."

She scrambles to me so eagerly, just like Truffle lurching towards her legs, the kitten held beneath her chin. And when Charlotte settles against my side, my arm draped around her shoulders, she lets out a tiny, blissful sigh.

It means nothing. It's comfort, nothing more. But that doesn't stop my chest from rioting. I lie there, rigid, cursing my own idiocy for thinking I could hold Charlotte like this and not let slip my feelings.

She's Parker's daughter. I clear my throat, shuffling to put half an inch between us. Charlotte's father and I have been friends since college; I was the best man at his wedding. If he saw us now—if he knew how greedily I breathe in her scent; how my blood heats to have her near—

"Alright. Better go back to your room," I rasp. But neither of us move. Charlotte scoots closer, resting her head on my chest, and Truffle marches across my abdomen.

"It's cold in there," she murmurs at last.

Fuck. Have I been neglecting her again? "I'll check the heating," I tell her quickly. "And we have spare blankets—"

"No, I mean. It's not that kind of cold. It's…" She pauses. Huffs a breath. "It's lonely."

My grip tightens on her shoulder. I shouldn't do it. I'll go straight to hell if I do—

"Sleep here, then." She hums and rubs her cheek against my chest, and God, if Truffle's tiny claws weren't kneading me I'd swear this was a dream. "Just for tonight."

"Thank you, James," she whispers, so quiet.

Goddamn it.

I'll never make it to morning.

Charlotte

I wake up curled on my side with a muscled arm banded around my waist. My back is warm, pressed against the ridges of a sculpted chest, and soft breath mists over my neck.

Oh wow.

James is…

He's holding me like he never wants to let go. Like no force on this earth could tear me from his grip, and holy crap, I *love* it. I've never felt so safe, so cherished. Never woken up so warm and comfy, my head well rested and clear, and my limbs all gooey and languid.

Mewl.

I squint one eye open, peering onto the bedroom floor. Truffle is attacking the bedside lamp cable, pouncing on the black wire and gnawing it with her pinprick teeth.

"Stop it," I hiss, trying desperately not to move. I don't want to wake James. The second I do, I know this moment will be over. "Haven't you done enough, you little menace?"

A deep voice rumbles through my hair. "Truffle's evil knows

no bounds."

I freeze, my heart pounding. But he doesn't pull away. Doesn't sit up and make excuses for the way we've woken twined around each other. If anything, James gathers me closer to his chest, holding me tight against his body.

Something prods at the small of my back. Something unmistakable.

Something that makes my mouth run dry.

"Did you sleep well?" I murmur, trying desperately to distract myself. If I let myself focus on the hard length pressed against my back, I'll do something reckless. Like reach behind with greedy fingers. Like rub myself all over it.

"Mm." James burrows his face in my hair, breathing deeply. And I lie there like an idiot, too stunned to move. The way he's acting—the things he's doing—

He doesn't *seem* like he finds me repulsive.

I lick my lips, wishing fervently that I could have brushed my teeth before he woke. But that would have meant untangling myself from his grip, leaving his warmth and his possessive hold.

I don't have that kind of willpower. Not even to hide morning breath.

I can feel the exact moment that James' brain catches up with his body. He goes rigid behind me, his hand stilling on my waist. His breath comes quicker against my neck.

"Charlotte? Fuck, I'm so sorry." Cold air washes against my back as he pulls away. He sits up, scrubbing at his face, as the bed covers pool in his lap. *"Fuck."*

I guess there's my answer. But my voice is surprisingly light as I sit up and swing my feet to the floor.

"No worries. It's natural, right? Instinctive. Um. I'd better shower." I scoop Truffle up, my cheeks flaming, and hightail it out of that room before he can see the downturn of my mouth.

He didn't mean it. Didn't mean *any* of it.

"You're in big trouble," I grumble at my kitten, once we're safely on the landing. I've never been so grateful to shut myself away in my cold, lonely room. I flop onto the bed, my neck still tingling from where his breath tickled me moments ago. "Don't ever do that again. You hear?"

She purrs at me, blue eyes bright, and sinks her claws in my arm.

* * *

I wish I could say things were normal in the office. That James was awkward, maybe, but polite and friendly. That he still called me on the intercom, summoning me to his room, and that he smiled at me on his way out at lunch time for his run.

I *wish* things were okay between us. But since this morning, James has not once met my eye.

"Men." I flick a balled up post-it note across my desk, grumbling to myself under my breath. You'd think from the clouds of guilt hanging around that man that we'd done something truly awful. Something unconscionable.

Is it really such a horrifying thought—that he might be intimate with me? I know I'm younger and kind of silly, well meaning but a hot mess. But I'm not a bad person. I pay my taxes; I help old ladies across the street. Hell, I have a stash of chocolate in my desk just for crying students.

Bleh.

James Gibson is going to break my heart. I know it.

"Knock knock." Leona leans in the doorway to my antechamber, her arms crossed over her chest.

"You can knock properly, you know. You don't have to say it."

Leona whistles, long and low, but she's not offended by my grouchiness. Her eyes crease with concern, and she strolls up to my desk.

"What's going on? Is it your parents again?"

"No." I tear another post it off the stack and crumple it into a ball. "No, they haven't called me lately."

I know how that sounds—like it would be a sad thing—but the truth is, the less my parents call me, the better. But it's so whiny, so lame, so I change the topic quickly.

"I'm viewing an apartment later."

"Nice! Want me to come with?" I start to say no, that James will come with me. But he won't even look at me right now, seems determined to pretend I don't exist, and I really *don't* want to go into an unknown building with a stranger alone.

"Yes, please."

"I could bring Mason too if you like? You know. Extra muscle."

How tragic. I need to borrow my friends' boyfriends for back up. But it's smart, so I nod again. "Sure. I'll get us coffees as a thank you."

"Oh!" Leona claps her hands, face lighting up. "Come over for a movie after. Everyone's going to be there."

I gnaw on the inside of my cheek. What's worse—third wheeling for three sets of couples? Or sitting at home in awkward silence with a man who won't look at me?

"Sounds good. I'll bring the popcorn."

Leona waves a hand. "Stop offering us stuff. We don't want gifts, we just want *you.*"

231

It's the nicest thing anyone has ever said to me. And I must be ovulating or some crap, because tears fill my eyes. Leona watches in horror as I suck in a shaky breath, scrabbling in my drawer for my box of Upset Student tissues.

"Oh shit. I broke you. Are you okay?"

"Uh-huh." I blow my nose, waving her away. "Apartment viewing. Movie night. That all sounds good. Thank you."

"Shall I fetch Dean Gibson—"

"No!" I squawk, horrified, just as the man himself steps into the doorway. He's back from his run, though you wouldn't know it by looking at him. His chest isn't heaving; his t-shirt isn't soaked with sweat. The only sign that he's been exercising at all is a faint sheen of perspiration on his forehead.

He takes one look at me and his face shutters.

"What happened?" he growls.

Leona glances between us, eyes wide. "I'll, um. I'll see you later, okay, Charlotte?"

"Yep." I wave her off. Please god, let this moment be over. "I'll text you the details."

"Charlotte," James warns, like I'm putting him off. Which, okay, I *am*, but only because for once, this is none of his business.

"I'm allowed to be sad," I tell him primly. "I'm on my lunch break."

"But—"

"I need to leave early," I interrupt. Better to get this over with; to rip off the band aid. "I'm viewing an apartment."

His shoulders slump. And damn it, he has no right to look so crestfallen. Like he'll actually miss me when I'm gone; like he *wants* me destroying his kitchen and sleeping in his bed.

"Is this because of Truffle?" he asks quietly. "Because I don't

232

care about the plates."

"No." I suck in a deep breath. And force myself to be brave and tell the truth. "It's because of you."

He jerks, like I've slapped him. And I hear it now, what that sounds like. As though I'm accusing him of something terrible, and that's not it at all.

"I've caused you so much trouble," I rush to say. "And I'm so grateful to you for letting me stay. But I can't keep getting under your feet. I mean, you wouldn't even *look* at me today. I don't want to ruin all the good things between us."

He's shaking his head, scowling, but I push my chair back and stand. "It's for the best. I'll, um. I'll be right back, Dean Gibson."

He flinches at his title, but I'm not trying to hurt him, damn it. I'm just trying to remind myself of my position here—I'm his assistant. His pesky lodger. And his best friend's daughter.

That's all I've ever be to James Gibson.

So I have to walk away.

James

Her key doesn't slide into the lock until after 9pm. I pause in the living room, where I've been wearing a hole in the carpet, pacing back and forth.

I know Charlotte's friend went with her to the viewing. But did she have to switch off her phone? I've been going insane with worry, gruesome images flashing before my eyes of Charlotte hurt or held captive by some maniac.

"What the hell?" I prowl forward as soon as she appears in the doorway, bundled up in her dove gray pea coat. Charlotte blinks at me, surprised, but there's no mistaking the shadows under her eyes. The tired slump to her shoulders.

I forcibly soften my voice. "Charlotte. Why didn't you call? I thought something might have happened to you at that viewing."

Her mouth forms an 'O', her hand twitching towards me, but she snatches it back. "Oh god. I'm so sorry. I didn't even think—I went to my friends' place to watch a movie."

My eyes drift closed, and the tension drains from my body.

Suddenly, I am bone-deep tired.

"Good." It's all I can manage. "As long as you're safe."

"I was. I am." She steps forward, timid, and with effort, I open my eyes.

She's blinding. So beautiful, I can hardly breathe. Maybe she's right—we shouldn't be around each other so much. Except the thought of not seeing her every day, of not wandering through the living room and seeing her curled on the sofa, painting her nails...

I can't bear it. Maybe I'm a monster, but I can't bear for her to leave.

"Turn down the apartment."

She snorts. "No fear. There were cockroaches in the bathroom." She's unwinding her scarf from around her neck, only half listening to me, dropping the pile of soft wool onto the coffee table. Truffle appears from nowhere, pouncing on the scarf's end.

"No, Charlotte. Listen to me. Don't view any others, okay? Stay here." I swallow. "Stay here with me."

"But..." She turns to me at last, those big blue eyes fixed solely on me. My battered heart flips over in my chest. "I can't stay here forever."

"Why can't you?"

She laughs, but it's more shocked than amused. "You don't want me here full time—"

"Yes, I do." I step closer. I can't help myself. I've been torturing myself for weeks, straining the last threads of my self control to make sure that I don't cross any lines. But since waking up with her in my bed, since seeing her eyes wet with tears in the office—my restraint has worn thin.

I'm dancing on a knife's edge. And suddenly I don't care

about what happens if I fall.

"Stay." My hand grips her elbow first. Then smooths up to her shoulder. And even through layers of fabric, I can feel her warmth. Her soft skin. "Don't look for anywhere else. Don't take yourself away from me."

"James," she whispers, something like hope dawning in her eyes.

This is insane. She's half my age. My assistant. My best friend's daughter. There are a thousand and one reasons why this can't happen, but right now, I've forgotten them all.

"Sweetheart." My head dips and I trace my nose along her hairline. She smells so fucking good, I want to bottle her and spray her on my pillow. "Please just tell me. Why were you crying earlier?"

Her fingers clutch at my waist, tugging my shirt. Pulling me closer. Closer.

"I… I don't…"

"Tell me." My command ripples over her. She shivers, legs wobbling where she stands.

"Leona said something nice to me."

"That's good." I make a mental note of her friend's face from earlier. If she needs anything at college, she can come to me. "What did she say?"

"That she doesn't want gifts from me. She just wants to be my friend."

I sort through that statement, turning it over in my mind. "Was that even in question?" It's nonsense. Of course Charlotte is enough on her own. She's the most charming person who ever popped into existence. She's *perfect*.

She gusts out a breath. "I guess not."

I hum. Nip at her earlobe. "*Definitely* not." She freezes, but not from fear—never mind her pulse tapping frantically in her throat. Charlotte is practically melting against me, begging for more contact, more sweet words from me, just *more*.

Why the hell have I been denying her this? Denying us *both*? I'm such a fool.

"Charlotte." My palm spreads over her back. Anchors her tight to me, so tight my heart slams against my rib cage trying to reach her. "I'm going to kiss you now."

"Oh." It comes out in a little squeak. "Um, okay."

"Tell me to stop." She shakes her head, mute, and tilts her chin up. Offers her sweet mouth; those plump, rosebud lips that have been haunting my nights. I stare at them, not willing to rush this moment, heat rushing under my skin.

"Please," she whispers, and that's it. My patience shatters, and my mouth crashes down on hers.

It's desperate. Longing. Tender, but with teeth. We grip each other tight enough to bruise, like we're both scared that the other will slip away. And how ridiculous that she's afraid of that—that she could possibly think I'd ever let her go. I was doomed from the moment I saw her at the airport, and feeling her crushed against my body has sealed our fate.

This is it.

I can never go back.

Her tiny whimpers make my cock surge to life. I want to wring those noises out of her again; I want her moaning, sobbing, *wrecked*. I've got a PhD, have been a professor in my time, but this will be the great study of my life—the study of Charlotte's pleasure.

"Charlotte." She scrapes her teeth over my throat and I groan. My hand plunges into her hair, wrapping her blonde locks around my fist. Not tight enough to hurt, but enough to take control. To boss her around, the way I *know* she likes.

"Charlotte," I snap, and the shudder than runs through her is so fierce, I feel it in *my* bones. She pauses, panting against my neck, her hands tugging so hard on my shirt the fabric might rip.

I don't care. She can rip what she likes. But first, I'll take her apart, piece by piece. I'll prove to her, once and for all, that I know exactly what her body needs. That no other man can make her feel like I can.

"Sit on the coffee table. Right in the center." Her feet trip over the rug as she hurries to obey. She still has her ankle boots and pencil skirt on, her stockings covering her legs and disappearing beneath the hem. Her cream blouse is rucked to one side, a flash of lacy lilac bra peeking through, and *fuck*.

Concentrate.

I don't speak again as I walk to her. As I kneel before her on the rug, undoing her boots with steady hands. To her, I must seem unruffled and calm. Barely affected by our kiss. But inside, I'm a maelstrom of emotion and hunger, a twisted mess of raw need.

I place her boots neatly to one side. Truffle tackles one immediately, knocking the boot over and spooking herself. She rockets into the kitchen in a ball of startled fur, and I smirk at Charlotte.

"It's for the best. I'd rather she didn't see this."

"See… what…"

She sounds dazed already, swaying where she sits. I kneel in front of her, placing a hand on either thigh, and nudge her legs open.

"Oh my god." Her eyes are glassy, fixed on mine.

"Close enough." I rub two small circles with my thumbs.

238

"Do you want to come, sweet girl?"

She nods so hard, her teeth rattle. Charlotte squirms closer, her legs bracketing my hips.

"I'll make you feel good." It's a promise. The most solemn oath I've ever taken.

"Please," she breathes. "I need it. I need you so bad."

I don't deserve this. No man could possibly deserve a declaration like that, but I'm a greedy bastard, so I'll take it. And guard it. This girl is *mine.* And I prove it to her, devouring her mouth and plunging my tongue between those lips.

Charlotte moans, sucking on my tongue, and I nearly blow right there. I pull back, resting my forehead against hers.

"What do you wear under these tight little skirts?" I creep one palm up the inside of her thigh, smoothing over the silken stocking. "I've been wondering. It's been driving me *insane.* Do you know how many times I had to bite down on my wrist, had to bring myself some fucking relief with you just next door?"

"No," she hiccups, squirming under my steady touch. "I d-didn't know that."

"Now you do." The crack of my other hand against her ass makes her jump; makes heat flood over her cheeks. I rub the same spot, soothing the sting away. "What would you have done if you'd known?"

"I'd have come into your office," she says at once, so fast it must be instinctual. "Come and knelt under your desk. Sucked—sucked you better."

"That's a good girl." Her reply has knocked the floor from under me, chased the breath from my lungs, but I don't let it show. My hand is steady as it slides higher up her thigh.

"*Oh.*" She screws her eyes shut, biting down on her lip

when my fingertips graze lace. She's hot and damp, her pulse practically throbbing through her panties.

"Do you want me to stop?" I ask through gritted teeth. I will if she tells me, though I might lose my sanity in the process.

"Don't you dare." She grabs at my shoulders, clutching my shirt as if to hold me in place. "I've—I've wanted this too—"

I can't hear anymore. Not if I want to do this right. So I hook her panties to the side, and run the pad of one finger along her seam, holding her in place by the hip as she bucks towards my touch.

"Easy," I murmur, delving between her folds. Finding the sensitive nub of her clit and teasing her there. She arches her back, her breasts pillowy against my chest, and I've never heard a sweeter sound than her whimpers.

She's slick.

Wanting.

So sensitive, she's on a hair trigger. I've barely slid two fingers inside her before she's twitching, clamping down on my hand, her muscles spasming as she comes. I work her through it, pumping in and out, teasing her clit with the pad of my thumb. And when she slumps against my shoulder, her flushed forehead resting on my collarbone, triumph curls my top lip.

"That's just the beginning," I promise her. "You'll beg for relief before I'm done with you."

"Uh-huh," she mumbles thickly, a lock of hair caught on her lip. She swipes it away as she sits up, eyes narrowed. "Let me—"

The doorbell rings as she reaches for my belt. We both freeze, too muddled to move.

"Who—" we both begin to speak at the same time. Then a

voice echoes through my front door down the hallway.

"James! Guess who's in the area, you old bastard?"

Charlotte stares up at me in horror.

Her father.

Charlotte

We couldn't have ruined the moment more if I'd thrown a bucket of icy river water over James. He lunges away from me at the sound of my father's voice, guilt and horror etched on his face. I watch him go, slumped on the coffee table like an abandoned doll. My skirt is pushed up my thighs; my cheeks are still warm from his embrace.

"Nice," I say flatly.

James comes back to himself. Scrubs a hand down his face then crouches in front of me, pulling my clothes gently back into place.

"I'm sorry. I—he took me by surprise. I thought he was on the other side of the country."

A hard lump is sinking through my insides. "No kidding."

"I just—I didn't expect—"

"No." I shrug him off, pushing to my feet and smoothing my skirt. "No, I guess you didn't."

So much for *stay here with me.* So much for that kiss. The first reminder he gets of my father, and James looks half sick with guilt. I don't want to see this. Don't want to watch the regret creep into his eyes. So I pat James on the shoulder on my way into the hallway.

"I'm going to my room. Tell Dad I've got a headache, okay? He'll be here to see you, anyway."

James doesn't argue with that. He saw what it was like for me growing up. My parents have always been more comfortable with their friends and colleagues than with me.

"Charlotte, wait."

I pause in the doorway, eyebrows raised. But he searches for the right words, his jaw clenching, then just shrugs, suddenly lost.

"It'll be okay. Alright, sweetheart? Just let me deal with your father."

I hum, rapping my knuckles on the door frame. I don't know why I ever thought it would go another way.

"Enjoy your catch up."

"Charlotte…"

"Goodnight, James."

My footsteps thump up the stairs, Truffle's little paws scrabbling behind me. And I keep my face carefully blank until I'm safely inside the guest room, where only my kitten can see me.

Then I flop on my bed, drag a battered paperback off my nightstand, and try to forget the last hour ever happened.

* * *

It's the worst night's sleep I've had since coming here. I go to bed way too early, before I'm even a tiny bit tired, and then I pay the price for it all night. I toss and turn, first too hot, then too cold, my previously comfortable mattress suddenly a lumpy nightmare. Shadows dance across the ceiling, Truffle snores lightly at the end of the bed, and all the while, muffled low voices drift up through the floor.

What are they talking about?

What did James mean when he said he'd 'deal with it'?

I huff, rolling over and smashing my cheek into the pillow. It doesn't matter. He'd never tell my father what we've done. Would never risk their decades-long friendship for a fling with a flighty young woman.

By the time the blue-tinged dawn light creeps around the edges of my curtains, I'm a basket case. I've been slipping in and out of sleep all night, fretting and grumbling and *sad*. Even Truffle's tiny snores couldn't cheer me up, and now I feel like death warmed over as I swing my legs out of bed.

Something tugs low in my belly. An ache. The constant reminder that James touched me somewhere sacred, that he wrung such intense feelings out of me that I forgot to breathe—then let me stomp upstairs, still wanting.

I didn't even get to touch him in return. To feel what he's *really* like beneath my palm, when I can explore his body without restraint.

I scowl at the wall, tugging my robe around my shoulders. Guess I'll never know.

There are voices in the kitchen when I finally drag my sorry ass downstairs. My skin is flushed pink from my scalding hot shower; my damp hair scraped back in a neat bun. There's nothing about me for my father to pick fault with this morning—as far as he knows, anyway—yet he still casts a critical eye over my dark pants and lilac blouse.

"What, you refuse to wear skirts to work now?"

That's the first thing he says to me. He hasn't seen me in *months.*

"Hello, Dad." I ignore his question, rounding the table and crossing to the refrigerator. James is leaning against the counter, his arms crossed as he fixes my father with a scowl. Parker Young and James Gibson—the world's oddest pair. My father is fair and ruddy where James is dark-haired and pale. Dad has softened in his old age, grown worn at the edges, while James looks ready to star in a Hollywood action movie.

Dad chuckles to himself, sat on an angle to the kitchen table. At least one of us finds him funny.

"What are you doing here?" My question comes out clipped. I hate that—I wanted to be cool. Unruffled. But the reminder that my father has barely spoken to me since I moved away is like rubbing sand in the wound.

He didn't even knock on my door last night. Did he ask where I was? Did it even occur to him?

"Last-minute meeting in the city." Dad snatches up his coffee mug, draining it in two gulps. "I always crash here, don't I James? It's a family trait."

He winks at me. I force a smile.

I'm being childish. This is ridiculous—nursing a grudge for my father's lack of interest when he's done so much for me over the years. So I take a deep breath, pour my own coffee, and sit opposite him. Offer a real smile this time.

"It's good to see you, Dad."

He grunts, cutting into a plate of bacon and eggs. I bet *this* is part of why he stays here, too—the freedom from Mom's strict wholegrain toast regime.

"How's your business going?" he asks, not even looking up. "Animal photos, wasn't it?"

Heat crawls up my throat. Damn it. *Damn it.* How is it that a few bored words from him can make me feel three inches tall? Can make all my plans and dreams feel suddenly stupid?

"Yes," I rasp. "Pet photography. It's going well, thank you. I've started a portfolio—"

Dad whistles. "A *portfolio*, eh?" He grins at James. The other man glares back. "Good thing you've got a real job to fall back on. Is this one working you too hard?"

"No," I snap. "Dean Gibson barely looks in my direction."

In the corner of my eye, James' head jerks towards me, the movement startled, but I glare down at the table as my dad roars with laughter.

"He's got better things to do, love," he wheezes at last, shaking his head at me fondly. And if I could sum up my relationship with this man, that sentence would be it.

He's got better things to do.

"Bullshit. I do not." James sounds angry. My dad pauses, glancing between us, and I can't do this. Not on twenty minutes of sleep.

"I'm going in early." My chair scrapes over the tiles as I stand up. "I already fed Truffle. I'll see you there, Dean Gibson."

"Charlotte—"

"Bye."

I hurry out before I say anything else. I don't trust myself not to make a horribly embarrassing scene—not to burst into tears or lash out at these two men who seem to like making me feel small.

"See you later," I whisper as I pass the kitten attacking the coffee table. Truffle pauses, blinking up at me with huge eyes. "Good girl." Her fur is soft beneath my fingertips, and my racing heart slows as I pet her before marching to the door.

246

Thank god for kittens. They're better than people, that's for sure.

* * *

My desk phone rings mid-morning. I clear my throat, dusting the crumbs from my coffee break cookie off my fingertips, and pluck the phone out of its cradle.

"Dean Gibson's office, this is Charlotte speaking. How may I help you?"

"Charlotte." My father's voice makes me stiffen. I dart a glance at James' office, but the door is sealed shut.

"Dad." I cough once, suddenly tongue-tied. "Um. Hi."

A long pause stretches between us. The rasp of his breath crackles down the phone, and I grimace at the polished surface of my desk.

"Shall I put you through to James?"

"No." He sniffs. "No, uh. I'm calling for you."

"Oooh-kay. How did the meeting go?"

"Good. Yes... Good." Wow. Is talking to your parents supposed to be this agonizing? I shift in my chair, ducking my head as a group of laughing students pass the open doorway. Their raucous voices echo behind them, loud enough for my father to hear.

"You're busy." He sounds relieved. "I won't keep you."

"Okay, I—"

"I apologize for this morning." The words sounds so alien coming from him. So stiff and rehearsed. I pull the phone away from my face and stare at it in my hand. The crackle of the handset brings it back to my ear. "I'm very proud of your business idea, Charlotte. You'll do fine."

This is a dream. A weird cheese dream. Or a product of sleep deprivation. I glance at the Dean's closed door again, narrowing my eyes.

"Did James…?"

Dad coughs. "He had a word once you left. Look, I'm—I'm sorry, sweetheart."

"That's okay," I tell him, my lips numb. I can't tear my eyes away from that door. "Did he use his angry Dean voice?"

Dad chuckles. "He did. He always could be a scary motherfucker." He cuts off quickly, realizing what he's said. But I'm already grinning, sliding lower in my seat.

"He makes the football players cry sometimes."

"Ha! I bet." Dad's voice changes suddenly. Gets serious again. "I hope he's not harsh with you?"

The memory of James clipping out commands in my ear, of him taking utter control over my body, the crack of his palm against my ass—it makes me *shiver*.

"No," I manage, voice strangled. "No, James is nice to me."

"Good. Well, uh. I'll see you later, sweetheart."

I hang up with a weird ringing in my ears. That's the longest conversation I've had with my dad in *years*. And he's definitely never apologized to me before—never spoken to me like an adult.

I bite my lip, glancing one last time at James' office. Then hiding a smile, I turn back to my work.

Charlotte

~⚬⚬⚬~

I get home late. I'm being kind of an ass, avoiding the house like this, but I don't want to ruin the fragile peace my father and I made over the phone. He may have gotten one of James' lectures, may be trying harder, but I don't want to tempt fate.

It was good. A nice conversation.

Let's leave it there.

Paige, Avery and Leona were more than happy to take me in, ushering me into their apartment with open arms. They fed me, made me hot chocolate, even made me watch a cheesy 90s Rom Com. As night fell, I was sorry to leave, trudging back onto the cold, wet street.

I had to come back, though. There's something… restless in me. A nervous, crackling energy shifting under my skin. Since my father got here, I've barely looked at James. Couldn't bear to see that guilt and regret in his eyes.

He's looked at me, though. I've felt the heavy weight of his eyes on me; the caress of his intense gaze running down my body.

I need to feel that again. I'm addicted, never mind the risks. So when I push the front door open, welcomed back into the warm glow of home, I don't scurry upstairs this time. I follow the sounds of low voices, the burst of my father's laughter, into the living room.

My father and James are on the sofa, two glasses of scotch on the coffee table. Truffle is on the rug, attacking my dad's shoelaces, and I'm glad to see at least *someone* is on my side.

"Hello," I murmur, shrugging off my coat. Two pairs of eyes turn to me—one sharp and one bleary.

"Charlotte!" Dad's voice is thick. He's must be deeper into the scotch than James. His friend watches me, sober and calculating, and there's something predatory in his gaze that makes my tummy flutter. "Did you get lost?"

"Nope." I bend down and scoop up my kitten, checking her over. She seems plump and happy, purring as I rub her against my cheek. "I went to a friend's."

"A boyfriend's?" Dad grins, waving a hand at the stony man beside him. "You'll have to keep an eye on her, James."

"I will." The low promise makes my toes curl in my boots. I risk a glance at James and find him staring at me openly, stark hunger and frustration sharpening his features.

"I'm, um. I'm going to bed," I whisper. Forget socializing. If I spend another minute here with him looking at me like that, I'll crawl into his lap and beg for a kiss, never mind that my father is right there.

"Sleep well," James says quietly. Dad misses it, already chattering about his meeting, but the way James says those words… it's clear he means something completely different. I swallow hard, my heart beating as fast as my tiny kitten's.

"Goodnight."

I flee upstairs, away from the thick tension crowding the air. Truffle squeaks, annoyed to be swept away so early, so I put her down and watch her bounce back down the stairs.

She's braver than me. Or more foolish. Either way, I dart inside my room and slam the door, heart slamming inside my chest.

* * *

This house is a classic build. Sturdy and powerful, just like James. But an older house comes with odd noises sometimes—the groan of settling floorboards. The rattle of a window blind.

I lay in bed, my skin heated beneath my borrowed t-shirt, my arms tossed over my head on the pillow. I listen to the gentle chorus of the house—the patter of tiny paws as Truffle runs riot in the living room; the muffled snores of my father on the sofa. The wind whistles against my bedroom window, the shadows of tree branches waving on the ceiling, and still he doesn't come.

Will he come at all?

Maybe he'll wait. Maybe that's all this will ever be—a dirty little secret between us, kept out of sight and out of mind. Perhaps he'll wait until my father is safely states away, and he can creep into my room without fear of being caught.

A footstep creaks on the landing outside my door. I hold my breath, straining to hear over the blood roaring in my ears.

The door handle turns slowly. It swings open on silent hinges. And James stands in the doorway, watching me, the moonlight casting his face half in shadow.

"I didn't want to wake you," he murmurs. His voice is so

deep, so velvety, that I shift on the mattress.

"I couldn't sleep," I whisper back, hoping he hears the invitation. The way I'm begging him to stay without saying the words. But something must finally be going my way, because James steps inside my bedroom and closes the door gently behind him.

"We'll have to be quiet," he warns.

"When we do what?" I grin, sitting up.

"Charlotte."

I roll my eyes. "Okay. My dad never has to know, if that's what you're worried about."

I can't keep the bitterness from my voice, the harsh edge. And James strides straight to the bed, lowering to sit beside my hip. He cups the side of my face, running his thumb over my cheek, and he sounds wrecked when he says, "Is that what you think? That I want to keep you secret?"

I nod, keeping my face carefully blank. Staring at a safe spot on his chest. He's wearing sweatpants and his black cotton t-shirt again, and they fit him so well it shouldn't be legal.

It's not fair. Couldn't he have a hump or something? Some kind of flaw, like the rest of us mere mortals?

"Charlotte. Look at me." I don't raise my eyes until he shakes me gently, and when I do, he traps me in his gaze. "You're not a secret. You're a gift—the best thing that's ever happened to me. I count myself lucky to have touched you at all." I swallow the lump in my throat, suddenly speechless, but he keeps going, his words urgent. "I don't want things to be messy so soon. I want it to be simple for a little while longer. But if you'd rather, I'll go downstairs right now and wake Parker up. Tell him you're mine."

I'm his. Maybe it's soon for him to declare that, but it feels

252

so *right.* It sings through my body; gives my heart wings.

My fingers wind in his t-shirt while he's speaking, anchoring me to this man. To this moment. And as soon as he stops to draw breath, I shake my head.

"No. Don't—don't do that. You're right. Let's keep it a secret a little while longer."

Because there's something else unsaid here. An electrifying thrill that comes from sneaking around—from the risk of getting caught together. And James must feel it too, because a growl rumbles in his chest as he crushes me close and kisses me. Hard. He slants his mouth over mine and devours me, taking me with every ounce of the possessiveness he's been holding back.

The slide of his tongue between my lips makes me whimper. I crawl closer, climbing into his lap like I wanted to downstairs, rocking the seam of my shorts against his hard length.

"Charlotte." He breaks off, breathing hard into my hair. I run my palm over the toned muscles of his heaving chest, marveling at the way I affect him. The way we affect each other. "Tell me, sweetheart. How far do you want this to go?"

"All the way."

He growls, a tendon standing out on his neck. I run a fingertip along it, then scratch at his beard.

"Think carefully," he grits out, his hands tight on my legs. "Once I get between these thighs…" He trails off, and I want to grab his handsome head and shake him. *Force* him to spell out exactly what he's going to do to me.

But the details don't matter.

"I'm sure." I wind my arms around his neck. Lean back in his embrace and roll my hips against his, drawing a ragged groan from between his gritted teeth. "I want it. I want *you.*" I swallow hard and lay all my cards on the table. Show him the dark desires that are shifting under my skin. "I can be quiet," I whisper. "My father never has to know."

James' eyes slam shut. He draws in a shuddering breath, then cups my elbow with one hand. His warm, dry palm slides up my arm, over my shoulder, up the side of my neck. He draws a line up the side of my body, and when he reaches the side of my face, he pauses, indecision creasing his brow.

I turn my head and kiss his palm. Give him the permission he needs. And all the air leaves his chest in a rush as James seals his hand over my mouth.

"Lie back."

I flop down on the mattress beside him, my limbs too jelly-like to be graceful. I do as he says, my eyes growing wide as he prowls on top of me, his big body trapping me against the bed, his broad shoulders blocking out the moonlight. My breath comes quick against his hand, but still he doesn't take it away. Instead, he reaches down between us and wrenches my shorts down my thighs.

"Soaked," he grits out, so damn satisfied. His fingers delve along my core, so proprietary, spreading the moisture gathering there. The truth is, I've been aching all day. Wanting him so badly from just outside his office. And now that he's touching me with those sure, firm hands, now that he's *pinning* me, blocking all sound from my mouth—

My hips rock up, urging him on. And James laughs darkly, lowering onto his elbow and trapping me even more.

"Don't worry, sweet girl. I'll give you what you need. I'll make you scream into my hand."

I pant harder, squirming, thrusting up into his touch, and he doesn't disappoint. He plunges two fingers inside me, filling me up and making my eyes roll back in my head.

"There you are. That's it, sweetheart." He croons to me, showering me in filthy praise as he takes me apart with his hand. His thumb finds my clit, teasing the bundle of nerves; his knuckles rub against my inner walls. He's stretching me, stroking me, *surrounding* me with his scent and his deep voice, and when I cry out, my hips lifting, my hoarse voice is muffled by his palm.

James waits for me to slump against the mattress. For me to lie boneless, heart rattling inside my chest. Then he pulls out his fingers slowly, holds my gaze, and licks them clean.

Oh god. I'm already squirming again. And his mouth quirks as he surveys me—a king surveying his subject.

"Delicious," he rasps, "so fucking sweet. And I'll lick you one day soon, Charlotte, but not tonight. I can't trust you to keep quiet, can I?"

I shake my head blearily. No. He can't trust me to do that. Not when the lightest stroke of his hands on my body makes me want to howl at the ceiling.

"That's right." James shoves my legs wider apart, settling his length against the crook of my thighs. He's still fully clothed, his sweatpants rasping against my bare skin, and I moan, arching up against him. "You're too far gone. So fucking needy for it, aren't you?"

I nod, frantic, gripping his wrist, but not to tug it away. To hold it closer to my face. And James' shadowed face is etched with savage satisfaction as he reaches between us, pulling his cock free. It lands against my pussy, sawing over the flesh, so heavy and burning hot, and *god*, I need that in me right now.

"Be quiet," he clips, and that harsh command sends shivers racing through my body. He's so tender one minute, so commanding the next, and the contrast makes my head spin. I want all of it—his gentle murmurs and the crack of his hand against my bare skin. The light kisses he drops of my forehead and the rough way he plunders my mouth other times, all teeth and tongue.

The broad head of his cock nudges my entrance. My hips twitch up, swallowing the first inch. And James curses loudly, never mind our little game. Never mind my father sleeping downstairs. He lets out a gravely string of curses, his hand tightening on my mouth, and thrusts deeper inside me.

"Mmph!" I cry out, just like he said I would. The stretch is intense—burning at first, then fading away as he pauses to let me adjust. His hips roll slightly, moving him inside me without pushing forward, and my groan comes from the back of my throat.

"More?" He's wearing thin. Barely restrained. His dark hair falls over his forehead, and his teeth are bared. I nod, writhing beneath him, trying desperately to help, and he grunts as he thrusts the rest of the way inside.

God. Oh god. This is—it's too much. It's too much and it's not enough, both overwhelming and a tease, and I cry out brokenly against his palm. James hushes me, kissing my closed eyelids as he begins to rock. Rolling his powerful body, *riding* me into the mattress.

"So fucking perfect." They're sweet words, but the way he spits them sounds angry. Moisture pools in my core, my nerves singing at his savagery. This normally calm, controlled man is falling apart. Brought to the brink of his control… by me.

I bite the palm of his hand, sinking my teeth into the flesh. And he inhales sharply, his hips moving faster.

"It's like that, is it?" My nails rake down his back and he grins at me, teeth pearly in the moonlight. He's moving faster, harder, rolling his body to hit the spots inside me that draw my moans. And I'm helpless beneath him, trapped in paradise, as he presses his bared teeth against my temple. "I know what you need."

Crack. His palm print stings against my ass. *Crack.*

He reaches higher, rucks up my stolen t-shirt, and twists my nipple. The sudden shock of pain sends me higher, my core ratcheting tighter, every nerve in my body singing out for more. I bite down harder on his hand, screaming hoarsely against his palm, and hitch my ankles behind his back.

It's nothing like when I've come before. There's no sudden clench, and then it's over. This is a maelstrom, a slow-building storm of sensations that buffets me in its winds. I cling to James, to his wrist, to his back, and spots float before my eyes as I twitch and moan with pleasure.

Sounds fade back in slowly. I'm slumped back against the mattress, my hair wild and my forehead damp. James kneels between my legs, his hand moving on his cock, and as he groans, wet warmth streaks across my bare stomach. I hold my stolen t-shirt out of the way, watching him paint me, hypnotized.

It's so primal. A man marking his territory.

And I should probably be offended, but honestly, it makes my knees weak. I *want* him snapping and growling over me.

I feel the same.

"Wait there." It's not a command this time. It's soft, so full of love that my stomach aches. James pulls his sweatpants back up and pads out of my bedroom, returning with a warm, damp cloth in his hand.

He cleans me up with tender hands. Pressing soft kisses to my stomach, my hip bone, my knee. And just when my heart is climbing into my throat, just when I think he's going to leave me here—

He tosses the cloth into the laundry basket and climbs into bed beside me.

"Get some sleep," he says gruffly, like he's embarrassed by his own display of tenderness. He pulls me against his chest, wrapping an arm tight around me.

"But…"

My dad could find us. This is such a risk.

"It doesn't matter." He's firm. "I'm not leaving, Charlotte. Now get some sleep."

I drift off with his lips against my neck, and his fingertips playing in my hair.

James

~~~~~~

At some point between Charlotte drifting off to sleep and the dawn light creeping around the curtains, something changed irrevocably inside me. Oh, I knew that I loved her. I've known that—been tortured by that realization—since approximately ten minutes after picking her up at the airport. But lying in bed with her in my arms, listening to the soft patter of rain on the sidewalk outside...

I'm a different man.

I slipped out of her room at first light, kissing her forehead and whispering my soft-hearted confessions into her hair. And I missed her like a phantom limb for the next hour, until she peeked shyly into the kitchen, her cheeks pink from the shower.

"Morning." She smiled at me over Parker's head. I vaguely noticed him staring at me oddly—no doubt my adoration for his daughter was written all over my face. But he didn't say anything, and we left him sitting at that table, preparing for his last meeting before heading back to the airport.

"You're being weird," she tells me now, an hour into our working day. I'm standing at her shoulder, theoretically reading the computer monitor over her head. In reality, I'm inhaling her sweet cherry scent and fighting the urge to bury my face in her lap.

"Am I? That's a shame."

A knock at the open doorway interrupts her retort. A bedraggled student stands clutching his satchel, a manic sheen of desperation in his eyes.

"Check your email," I murmur to Charlotte, squeezing her shoulder before leading this latest cry for help to my office. She raises an eyebrow at me as I pull my door closed, clicking with her mouse.

It's a good thing. At least, *I* think it is. I hope she thinks so too when she sees what I've sent—a list of openings in other campus offices that I could recommend her for. Not that I don't love having her around all day, not that I don't *crave* her presence like a starving man staring at a buffet.

But she already lives in my house. I can't be her boss too, not anymore. I want her with me because she *wants* to be, because she's as crazy about this as I am. Not because she's trapped.

"Is there anything you can do?" the student sniffles, dragging me back to reality. And thank god at least part of me was listening, because I rattle off our options without a pause.

I try and fail for the next hour to put Charlotte out of my mind. I resolve the student's issue; I wade through mounds of paperwork; I plan for the next academic year. And though I can't honestly claim to stop thinking about her, I at least don't move from my desk until I hear voices in the antechamber.

The hairs rise on the back of my neck. And I push to my feet, rounding the desk quickly.

"I'm just saying, honey." Parker leans against Charlotte's desk, towering over where she stares at him, flushed and unhappy. "There's no shame in coming home. You've always needed a bit of extra help, haven't you? We can't give you that while you're here."

I wait in the doorway for Charlotte to speak. For her to stand up for herself. But she's too taken aback, hurt sparkling in her eyes, and I can't fucking stand it anymore.

"Charlotte doesn't need help." I stride across the room. Come to face Parker, my arms crossed over my chest.

He stands, his smile fading. "Yeah. I see that. Because *you're* giving it to her, is that right?" His tone is lewd, loaded with innuendo, and Charlotte flinches. Blushes brighter.

"No." It's an effort to keep my voice level. To not rail off and punch the man I've known for decades. "I said she doesn't *need* help. She's fully capable. She's a smart, creative woman."

Parker scoffs. "She's a ditz."

"Dad!" Charlotte's pissed off, finally, launching up from her chair, but not before I've reeled off and punched my best friend in the face.

It's a tactical blow. Aimed for his cheekbone, not his nose. No permanent damage done—just a warning delivered.

A final warning.

I won't have that shit in my earshot. *No one* talks about Charlotte like that, least of all her fucking parent. I shake out my hand, wincing at the sting, but I'm not sorry. I'd do it again. I'd do it a thousand times to stand up for her.

"James," Charlotte murmurs, and my blood cools slightly. I step back, breathing hard, and give her some space. Charlotte turns to her shell-shocked father where he clutches his reddened cheek, staring at the two of us.

"That was very rude," she says, clear and controlled. Everything I'm not right now. "Don't speak about me like that, please. If—if you do, I won't want to see you." Her cheeks flush brighter, shocked by her own daring, but she pushes on, hands balled into fists at her sides. "Also, I'm with James. We're together. And—and if you can't be polite about it, you can't come to stay anymore."

Parker's eyes swing to me. Betrayal swirls in their depths, but there's something else. Bitter acceptance.

Something tells me I lost a friend today. It doesn't matter. Charlotte is worth it.

She's worth everything.

"Fuck this," Parker mutters, turning on his heel and pushing out into the crowded hallway. Charlotte watches him go, dismayed, while I watch her carefully. Scanning for signs that I fucked up; that I pushed this too far. And when she finally turns to me, arms reaching, I tug her gratefully against my chest.

"I'm sorry," I murmur into her hair. "I turned into a bit of a caveman."

She makes a weird sound—part laugh, part sob—and cuddles closer. "I don't mind. It was kind of nice."

A few students do a double take as they pass the open doorway.

"People will stare," Charlotte mumbles. She's right—here's the college Dean, his arms wrapped tight around his much younger assistant as she sniffles into the front of his shirt. The rumors will spread like wildfire—there will be no escaping the gossip.

She starts to move back, but I hold Charlotte tighter.

Screw it. What's a rumor or two?

"Come with me." I draw her back towards my office. Away from the peeking eyes and straining ears. Charlotte comes with my easily, clutching my shirt, an excited flush already tinting her cheeks.

"What are we going to do in there?"

"Oh, sweetheart." I tug her close, the next words just for her. "What *aren't* we going to do?"

Charlotte

Three years later

I adjust Truffle's bow tie, picking bits of fluff off her cushion. The lamplight makes her brown fur extra glossy; brings out the deep hue of her gorgeous blue eyes.

She's still my star. Even now, when I have a full roster of clients, and there's a waiting list for my photo shoots. Truffle is the one everyone wants to see—the one who goes viral and makes the whole internet fall in love.

"Smile," I mumble, pressing the shutter. My camera clicks and whirs, taking photo after photo of my cat as she stares back at me, so freaking smug.

Yeah, she knows she's gorgeous. Truffle's kind of a brat. But she's *my* brat, and I need to give her all my love at the moment. In a month's time, she won't be my only baby anymore. My belly is swollen under my shirt—another one stolen from my husband—the skin hyper-sensitive to every brush of fabric.

"Is she behaving?"

His low voice makes me smile. Makes my insides go all tingly. Even now, he has this effect on me—makes me lose my train of thought. On the cushion, Truffle perks up and starts preening.

I'm not the only one with a crush.

"Minimal destruction so far." I smile over my shoulder. Truffle is the clumsiest cat in existence. James leans in the living room doorway, his dark shirt unbuttoned at the collar. He looks so good, so crisp and manly, and I bite my lip. His eyes darken.

"Your father called." He strolls forward, hands in his pockets. "He asked me to tell you he loved yesterday's shoot. Apparently your mother has already ordered prints."

I smile down at my camera. It took a while, but when my parents saw my business take off, when they saw how popular it is, they came around.

I'd have kept going either way, but it still feels good. Especially when a hard chest presses against my back, two strong arms winding around my middle.

"Should you be on your feet?" he murmurs against my neck.

I snort. "Why? Should I be on bed rest for the next month?"

"If you like." His beard tickles my throat, his lips tracing up to my jaw. "I could rub your feet. Bring you breakfast in bed."

"That does sound pretty good." I flick through the photos on my camera. "Living the Truffle lifestyle."

"Soon it'll be sleepless nights and throw-up on our shirts," he warns. But he can't hide the excitement and longing in his voice, and I tip my head back against his shoulder. He's sturdy and warm behind me. Always my rock.

"You're excited," I whisper. "Don't be a grouch."

"Very excited." His hands smooth over my belly. Grip my

hips. "You're stuck with me forever now, sweetheart. You're *mine*."

"I was already yours!" I splutter, but he's taking my hand. Placing the camera on the coffee table and leading me to the doorway. Our footsteps creak on the stairs and I grin at the back of his shirt as my husband leads me to our bedroom.

Maybe he'll rub my feet. Maybe he'll rub other things.

Either way, I'm his. And he's *mine*.

* * *

Thanks for reading the Teacher's Pet collection! I hope you loved the girls and their tormented men. For more time with them, check out the series bonus epilogue—it's Avery's and Leona's graduation. And all four couples manage to slip away...

& For more sweet and steamy box sets, check out Wild Obsession for rugged men in the wilderness, and Seeing Double for twin swap antics.

xxx

Cassie Mint

About the Author

Cassie writes outrageous, OTT insta-love with tons of sugar and spice. She loves cookie dough, summer barbecues, and her gorgeous cat Missy.

You can connect with me on:
- https://www.authorcassiemint.com
- https://www.bookbub.com/authors/cassie-mint
- https://www.amazon.com/~/e/B08VF8BPWG

Subscribe to my newsletter:
- https://www.authorcassiemint.com/newsletter